M000023952

Hallow Be the Haunt

Also From Heather Graham

Please look for Heather's Mira Krewe of Hunters Novels!

Hallow Be the Haunt

A Krewe of Hunters Novella

By Heather Graham

1001 Dark Nights

EVIL EYE
CONCEPTS

Hallow Be the Haunt
A Krewe of Hunters Novella
Copyright 2017 Heather Graham Pozzessere
ISBN: 978-1-9459-2045-5

Foreword: Copyright 2014 M. J. Rose

Published by Evil Eye Concepts, Incorporated

All rights reserved. No part of this book may be reproduced, scanned, or distributed in any printed or electronic form without permission. Please do not participate in or encourage piracy of copyrighted materials in violation of the author's rights.

This is a work of fiction. Names, places, characters and incidents are the product of the author's imagination and are fictitious. Any resemblance to actual persons, living or dead, events or establishments is solely coincidental.

Sign up for the 1001 Dark Nights Newsletter
and be entered to win a Tiffany Key necklace.

There's a contest every month!

Go to www.1001DarkNights.com to subscribe.

As a bonus, all subscribers will receive a free
1001 Dark Nights story
The First Night
by Lexi Blake & M.J. Rose

One Thousand and One Dark Nights

Once upon a time, in the future…

*I was a student fascinated with stories and learning.
I studied philosophy, poetry, history, the occult, and
the art and science of love and magic. I had a vast
library at my father's home and collected thousands
of volumes of fantastic tales.*

*I learned all about ancient races and bygone
times. About myths and legends and dreams of all
people through the millennium. And the more I read
the stronger my imagination grew until I discovered
that I was able to travel into the stories... to actually
become part of them.*

*I wish I could say that I listened to my teacher
and respected my gift, as I ought to have. If I had, I
would not be telling you this tale now.
But I was foolhardy and confused, showing off
with bravery.*

*One afternoon, curious about the myth of the
Arabian Nights, I traveled back to ancient Persia to
see for myself if it was true that every day Shahryar
(Persian: شهریار, "king") married a new virgin, and then
sent yesterday's wife to be beheaded. It was written
and I had read, that by the time he met Scheherazade,
the vizier's daughter, he'd killed one thousand
women.*

*Something went wrong with my efforts. I arrived
in the midst of the story and somehow exchanged
places with Scheherazade – a phenomena that had
never occurred before and that still to this day, I
cannot explain.*

Now I am trapped in that ancient past. I have taken on Scheherazade's life and the only way I can protect myself and stay alive is to do what she did to protect herself and stay alive.

Every night the King calls for me and listens as I spin tales. And when the evening ends and dawn breaks, I stop at a point that leaves him breathless and yearning for more. And so the King spares my life for one more day, so that he might hear the rest of my dark tale.

As soon as I finish a story... I begin a new one... like the one that you, dear reader, have before you now.

Prologue

David Henderson laughed as the cadaverous witch danced before him. The person—actor or actress or just-out-for-dress-up-fun person— was really magnificent. The costume was tight and black, with some kind of extra piece flowing around the body. The hat was big and black and pointed. The face... The face was the best. Green and mottled, with a huge hooked nose. And the eyes burned in a mixture of red and gold. Fantastic!

Annoying, though. David knew that the house just outside the French Quarter off Frenchmen Street was occupied that night only by one person, the old man who had owned it for years and years. His family had recently refurbished the home, which had been in a sorry state since the devastation of Katrina. But now, the old man's Wall Street son-in-law had been pouring money by the gallon into the place. It was prime for picking.

Or, in David's case, prime for the robbing.

And if the old man gave him any trouble?

That's why Tink Aldridge was working with him.

Tink wasn't against violence in any form. They wouldn't set out to kill the old guy. He was just old. But if he got in the way...

Maybe he wouldn't. David was no sadist. Maybe Tink was, just a little bit. Didn't matter. There were riches to be had in that place, and David—who delivered pizza to the house—happened to know that the old man's daughter, son-in-law, and their little brat-boy were gone for the week. Back to New York City to take care of some business there. It was a good thing to be able to hang around and smile and wait patiently for the few dollars they scrambled for to pay for their pizza. It gave him time to learn those little tidbits.

And figure out how to rob the family dry.

"Sacrifice, son. Sacrifice," the witch cackled.

She shook her broomstick at him, like something out of a bad horror movie.

He was thinking it was too bad he didn't have a pup with him so she could cry out she'd get his little dog, too.

"What the hell?"

David realized Tink had arrived. They'd made a point of meeting here, just off Frenchmen. While the pulse that came from the many music venues on Frenchmen Street was loud, here the sound was muffled—and the street usually deserted.

"It's a witch," David said, looking at Tink.

It was good Tink was here. He was a frigging giant. Six-five, built like brick. Nice for him—since he did have his sadistic tendencies. Good for David tonight. No one messed with Tink. Not for long.

"It's an ass," Tink said dryly. He pointed. "Being joined by other asses."

And Tink was right. Two more witches had appeared. They were identical—down to the tips of their black hats and the curve of their giant noses—and red and gold, evilly gleaming eyes.

They swayed for a moment and then stood dead still, staring at Tink and David.

"Bunch of jerks. Get off this sidewalk—or I'll wipe the old gum off it with your noses," Tink said.

The witches stared at them for a second and then began to cackle. Tink shook his head. He called out a number more names—"cunts" was among his more colorful—and then started to stride over to them.

The first witch stepped out from the group.

Tink headed straight for her.

He was about to deliver one of his debilitating right hooks to the jaw—but his fist never connected.

The witch ducked low, and then jerked up.

David stared in bewilderment, and then in horror as Tink turned to him.

Tink's eyes were wide with disbelief. His hands were at his throat, clutching it as if he was choking.

As if...

He *was* choking. Blood spurted from him in a flow of crimson that wasn't to be believed, that couldn't be real.

It was almost Halloween. It was a trick.

But it wasn't.

Tink took a few steps, staggering with his massive bulk and height.

And then he went down. Just like a giant redwood sawed at the root.

Again, for a moment, David just stared. Shocked.

Then he realized the witches were silent. And they were looking at him.

From Frenchmen Street, the pulse of drumbeats could be heard, softened to a strange thrum by the distance.

A saxophone played, also muted and plaintive.

The witch who had just felled Tink took a step forward.

David stared a split second longer. Then he turned and ran.

Ran for his life.

He heard their cackling laughter. And he prayed it would soon fade like the distant sound of the drum.

Chapter 1

Donegal Plantation sat back on Louisiana's River Road, a grand dame—regal, elegant, and glorious. She was an icon of days gone by. Good days and bad days, certainly. For she had been built in the sweeping Colonial Southern style, and she immediately brought to mind a time of hoop skirts and mint juleps.

Grandeur—and cruelty.

Cotton had been king in the South, and while the Donegal family had been famous for their kind treatment and for allowing slaves to earn their freedom, slavery had still existed here.

To many the plantation was a fascinating glimpse at the days when the country was in turmoil, days when slavery had existed, when the prevalent mindset had longed for riches more than the freedom and equality of man.

To others, she was a spellbinding curiosity.

And to this day, despite political controversy, she offered up a re-enactment of a long-ago skirmish during which, history had shown, it hadn't been war or ideals, but the jealousy and cruelty of one man which had brought about the death of the most famous member of the family.

Captain Marshall Donegal.

He and his beloved wife had been the main ghosts of the great house for decades, though sightings of them had ebbed in the last few years.

Rumor—cruel rumor—had even stated that Emma Donegal had killed her husband, furious with him for his infidelities. Except that there hadn't been any infidelities, and eventually, the truth had been proven.

Donegal Plantation was beautiful. It echoed the glory and the agony of history. Now a museum, it was often used as a guesthouse as well. But for the month of October, no rooms were rented out. It was simply too crazy a time.

And, at the moment, Donegal Plantation was "haunted."

Not just in reality. But also commercially, for the Halloween season.

An early 1800s hearse sat in the sweeping drive. The striking white pillars at the entrance were draped in black. Menacing witches on broomsticks were hung here and there along the antebellum porch—along with ghosts, goblins, and evilly grinning jack-o'-lanterns.

Driving up to the house, Ashley Donegal smiled—and let out a sigh at the same time. Donegal Plantation was her home. She loved it—fiercely. She was proud of the property. They had a re-enactment each year of the Civil War skirmish that had been fought here. And they laid it all out for the truth of what had been.

The good that had occurred.

And the bad.

Her grandfather, Frazier, was still alive. And, with the help of his employees Beth and Cliff, he kept Donegal plantation going with tours and events—such as Halloween.

So it was right and good that she was now on this trip to plan her wedding to Jake Mallory. It was here—years ago—her ancestor's death had been proven to be a murder, not just an act of war. And it was here where they had solved the murders that had taken place then.

The murders that had brought her and Jake back together again.

She had been in love with Jake as long as she could remember. But it hadn't been until her father's death that Jake, a member of an elite unit of the FBI, had come back.

And they had been together ever since.

What had caused them to take so long to marry, she wasn't sure. Probably because it hadn't really mattered. They were together. But recently, they'd talked family. And in talking family...a wedding seemed the thing to do.

And if they were going to have a wedding, it was going to be at Donegal Plantation.

Now, in between the crazy Halloween tours and everything else, she was going to meet with her grandfather and Beth and plan her wedding. Her mom, long gone now, had dreamed of such an event.

Her father, also gone many years, had thought it would be a grand idea. The plantation would be the perfect venue. And they could put up just about everyone who would come, which would be the majority of the Krewe of Hunters—Jake's very elite team. Those who could get away, because the office could never be empty. There was never a time when they weren't needed, even though the "unit" had grown by leaps and bounds and there were now more than twenty-five special KOH agents.

Naturally, she and Jake came back for the re-enactment every year. At one time, Ashley had been prominent in the planning of the event—the vendors, the tents, the history chats by visiting professors, the players in the skirmish themselves. In more recent years she hadn't been as involved, and she missed being part of the history and education of the times gone by. She was proud that, despite everything that had happened there, the plantation continued with its traditions.

And though their home was now in Alexandria, Virginia, due to the Krewe, Donegal Plantation—and her grandfather—remained a major part of their lives.

* * * *

It was late when she arrived back home that night. She'd had a meeting with a professor in New Orleans who was going to take part next year in the re-enactment. She had been there for a few days already, but Jake had just flown in that afternoon.

She was anxious to see him, but before she went in, she paused to survey the house and grounds. They kept floodlights on by the door, and she could see the sweep of the lawn stretching ahead of her between the main house and the stable entrance. She thought, looking at the beauty of the surrounding oaks and the cemetery, they would have the reception out on the lawn, with the wedding inside, in the grand foyer. Her grandfather could walk her down the sweeping stairway and give her away.

It would all be just as her parents had envisioned long ago.

She hurried up the stairs and could already hear Jake in the kitchen, speaking with Beth Reardon, who managed the house. She glanced in quickly. Jake was talking security features and didn't notice her presence.

Ashley slipped by and hurried into her room. She and Jake had been apart less than a week, and she was feeling excited–and a bit mischievous—now that he'd arrived.

She quickly showered, dried off, and donned one of her favorite robes.

Silk.

Soft as a whisper against her flesh.

In just seconds, Jake came into her bedroom.

He'd been an amazing boy—eight years old to her five—when they'd first met. Their parents had been friends.

And he'd been a tall, strapping teenager when they'd first fallen in love.

Her own fear of herself and life and death had come between them, but when murder had occurred at Donegal Plantation, she had seen him again.

He'd become the kind of man who automatically drew attention. Tall and broad-shouldered, perfectly fit. Dark and handsome.

But it wasn't his appearance that had always called out to Ashley. It was a certain confidence in the way he lived, in the integrity that existed not just in his mind, but in his life and in his deeds.

"Thought you'd slip by me?" he teased.

"I didn't want to interrupt you and Beth. You were meeting with one of the most beautiful women I know—in your robe." She was teasing. Beth was beautiful, tall and exotic, from her dark skin to her mammoth eyes—and down to her soul as well. She had been born in Jamaica, and had come to Orleans Parish as a young adult. She'd fallen in love with Donegal Plantation when Ashley's parents had been looking for someone to work in the house.

They had all fallen equally in love with Beth.

Jake didn't take her seriously. He grimaced. "I'd showered. She thought you were back already. And I know that I'm almost irresistible in terry." He smiled roguishly. "But I was waiting for you." He motioned to the window. "Hot afternoon once I got here; went riding with Cliff to make sure the property was all good—what with Halloween and everything. I saw ads driving out." He chuckled. "I forgot how crazy Donegal gets at Halloween."

She grinned. "Taxes, maintenance, keeping the staff. We have to go a little crazy."

"I know." He moved to her. "And I love coming out for this. I'm just lucky I'm able to get the time."

The Krewe of Hunters never ceased to amaze Ashley. She'd been stunned to realize it was possible for the human soul to remain—and that ghosts did exist. Now, after so many years, she took it in stride. She'd wasn't a part of the Krewe; she'd become a tour guide in Alexandria, a city she had come to love with all her heart as well. That allowed her the freedom to come home as needed.

But she knew the Krewe well, from the original six members to the many who had joined since. And so she was aware that there was a host of people in the world who knew that the spirits of the dead could linger. Sometimes for help, and sometimes waiting because they might be needed. Sometimes, they went on. And sometimes they stayed, because they felt their presence was necessary.

She forgot the Krewe then, because Jake was holding her. She smiled and said softly, "It's a beautiful night."

"It is."

"And… There's nothing to mar it."

He grinned at that. "Jackson will only call me if absolutely necessary, and with the Krewe we now have…"

She nodded and stepped away. The drapes were still open.

French doors allowed one to walk out on the wraparound balcony and look over the expanse of the property, all the way out to the graveyard, which boasted some of the finest funerary art in the country. The view offered more—beautiful night skies, the moon, the stars, and the sweet scent of the magnolias and other flowering trees.

She had been there for just a moment before she felt Jake's presence, and then he was wrapping his arms around her.

She'd known he would follow.

"It's going to be beautiful," he whispered, pulling her back against his body.

She turned, looking at him. "I guess it did take us a while," she whispered. "And… It will be beautiful. It wouldn't matter though. I've known forever that I'd never want to be with anyone else for the rest of my life."

"I'd have no life without you."

She grinned. "God, you have quite a way with words."

He smiled in turn. "So do you."

He kissed her lips. Softly at first, and then more passionately.

Jake had a way of kissing. Teasing to start. The pressure of his lips gradually increasing. Adding his tongue with a promise of so much else...

He lifted her up into his arms. "I feel like we've been married forever."

"Oh, good Lord, you don't mean it's getting old?"

"It's always brand new for me," he assured her.

They went back in and he set her down for a moment, hands sliding beneath the shoulders of her silk robe.

She stilled his movement. "Not that I think anyone is lurking around the porch, but..."

He quickly closed the drapes and came back to her, hands on the silk robe again, sliding it to the floor this time.

"You're beautiful," he told her.

"Your words are good. Very, very good," she said, and pulled at the belt of his robe, repeating his action. Silk and terry seemed to tangle on the floor, as if the robes themselves were entwined in passion.

She stepped back a moment and smiled. "You really are beautiful too."

He laughed, swept her back into his arms, and laid her on the bed, falling beside her. "Brand new," he whispered. "Like the first time I touched you." He caressed her cheek. "Except I anticipate it more than ever now." He stroked down her neck. "Because what might have existed in my imagination for so long can never compare to what I know to be real."

He kissed her again and then maneuvered her to the side to lift her hair and kiss the back of her neck. Then lower and lower and lower, until his mouth brushed the small of her back. He turned her again, his kiss, his touch so intimate that she stifled a cry as she reached down, drawing him back up. Their mouths met with urgency and hunger, hot and very wet. She twisted in his arms, her mouth free again, and delivered kisses all over his skin. Marveling at the tautness of it, at the sleek muscles he'd built up in order to be the best possible agent in the field... And because that was Jake.

Physical.

Wonderful.

She teased him until he let out a hoarse cry, then their lips connected again as he moved over her. And then into her.

And she was in awe that he was right. Everything was perfect.

Each time they made love.

His flesh became as slick as her own. A feeling built inside her, one that she wished would last forever. And yet urgent, so urgent. Building like the storms that sweep over Southern skies. As potent, as tempestuous.

Moving... Reaching... Arching... Writhing...

And then stars to match those outside seemed to swim before her eyes.

Jake, breathing at her side, his heart beating like the drums on Bourbon Street...

"Hmm. Think we should have waited until we were married?" he laughed.

She hit him with a pillow.

"It would have been one hell of a wait," she told him.

He laid back with a contemplative look. "Married, though. I like it."

And, snuggling against him, she agreed.

They were home—or, at least, the place that would always be home in Ashley's heart. It was a good feeling. A safe one.

So they made love again. And then once again.

And with the extreme intimacy between them, which had only grown over time, they slept.

But maybe it was that—being home. Home. Here. Donegal, where the dead had first entered her dreams.

Because as Ashley slept, she began to dream again.

She wasn't at the plantation. She was an hour away, in the heart of New Orleans. Walking down Bourbon Street.

She seldom headed to Bourbon Street, the commercial heart of the French Quarter. She usually had friends playing Uptown, or in the Garden District, on St. Charles or Magazine Street. She had nothing against the bars and strip clubs and all else that existed in the Quarter. In fact, she particularly loved Lafitte's Blacksmith Shop, now a bar. A touch of history from the time when pirates had ruled the city—and helped to save it and the country from the massive power of Great Britain. But even so, she rarely visited.

And still, she walked.

Maybe she was headed down from Canal toward Esplanade, perhaps on her way to Lafitte's. She could see partiers in the street.

Some wide-eyed, some slightly staggering, having been, perhaps, just a wee bit over-served. She could hear the music coming from a dozen bars, each vying to have the loudest, best, most enticing entertainment. Hawkers vended beer and spirits on the sidewalks in front of a few of the establishments, and scantily clad women stood at dark doorways, enticing many to enter their dens of desire and...dance.

A young woman suddenly appeared before her.

"Please," she whispered.

The girl had to be in her early twenties. She had long, golden hair and enormous brown eyes. A pretty face, with round cheeks and a generous mouth. She seemed incredibly distressed and Ashley stopped walking. She looked around for one of the mounted policemen who patrolled the Quarter, but she didn't see anyone who resembled law enforcement or security.

"Can I help you? Do you need a ride? Are you lost?" Ashley asked worriedly.

The girl shook her head. Giant tears appeared in her eyes.

"Please, please, help me," she said. She reached out, as if she would touch Ashley's face, as if she was desperate for human contact.

"I'm happy to help you. But what's wrong? I can't help if I don't understand the problem."

"You must... You must... You see me here... Please..."

From somewhere, a chorus from a "Journey" song became loud. The sounds of the revelers on the street suddenly seemed like a cacophony.

And then the young woman gasped. "They're coming!"

"They? Who?" Ashley turned to see what had so distressed the girl.

There was darkness. Like a flock of ravens, or a massive ball of dark mist. Or storm clouds making their way down the street.

"Please," Ashley heard the whisper and turned back.

But the young woman was gone.

What in God's name?

Ashley turned again. The mist was coming. She felt it as it came closer. It did look like a whir of raven-dark wind, or the sky when a bad storm threatens. And it moved, sweeping down the street. And in it, she sensed...

Danger. Malignance.

Evil.

She wanted to turn and run. It was coming closer and closer.
Coming for her.

Then she heard something, something different from the music of Bourbon Street, from the laughter of the ever-so-slightly inebriated, the hawkers, the vendors, the chatter, the neon...

It was a sharp sound.

And she woke with a start.

It was Jake's cell phone. He'd answered it, sitting up on the bed.

She knew he was speaking with Jackson Crow, field supervisor for his special division within the bureau.

And also, she knew.

She knew the young woman in her dream had been murdered.

And the ghost of the girl had come to her.

Chapter 2

"Witches?"

Jake Mallory had been through many different situations since he'd first joined the Krewe of Hunters.

But he'd never received a call about *witches* before.

Over the phone, Jackson's voice was no-nonsense, as usual. "Curious case," he said. "First, they found a young woman—a local named Shelley Broussard—and she'd had her throat slit. But she wasn't killed where she was found—just outside St. Louis #1. She'd been set down on the street as if she was drunk and passed out. There was no blood; she was obviously killed elsewhere and then displayed there. She had a sign hanging around her neck. It read *Traitor*. And she had a cup by her side—as if she'd been begging." He paused. "Actually, a few kindhearted people had put some change and a few bills in her cup before one of the onlookers realized she was dead and called the police."

"Murder is always a tragedy." As Jake knew well. "But Jackson, that's one for the NOPD. They aren't going to want us butting in. And what does this have to do with witches?"

"There was a second murder—last night. A hood. He had his throat slashed." Jackson sighed. "Now I know it's a lot of supposition, Jake, but the medical examiner suggests the young woman and our hood were killed with the same weapon. It's a hard thing—unless you have the right blade—to easily slit a throat to that extent. No butter knife was used, that's for sure. Anyway, the thug was found on the street right where he was murdered. Just outside the French Quarter, near Frenchmen."

"Witches, Jackson, really? Where do they come in? It is nearly

Halloween. But—"

"There was a witness to the thug's murder. Another thug. He saw the witches—first one, and then three. They were posturing in the street. His friend joined him. The man killed was a 'Tink,' or Thomas Aldridge. Big guy—a good six-five, shoulders of steel. His buddy— totally hysterical, according to Detective Isaac Parks, lead on the case for the NOPD—admitted that the two of them were going to break into a newly refurbished house and rob the place blind. He wants to stay in jail. He's afraid to go back out on the streets of New Orleans."

Jake realized Ashley had awakened. She was watching him. He winced. They had come to plan specifics on the wedding, and instead he was talking shop.

But she was watching him gravely. And he knew again why he loved her so much. Ashley didn't need continued assurances; she didn't hesitate for a minute when work interfered with something they had planned.

She saw the dead herself; the Krewe had solved a murder right here. But that wasn't it. Ashley was just...Ashley. And he loved everything about her, including her mind, her soul, her integrity—and her heart.

"Hang on," he told Jackson. "Ashley is with me. I'm going to speakerphone."

She smiled at him and scooted closer.

Jake had a feeling his boss would welcome the help. Jackson knew Ashley well. And while she wasn't Krewe, she was one of "them"—the gifted. Sometimes the cursed.

"So, this thug—who saw Tink murdered and escaped, running like the wind—says in the end, there were three witches. Tink, he admits, meant to smash the witches to the ground. But after Tink approached one and turned back around, he was spurting blood from here to eternity. Bottom line, Isaac Parks is waiting for you in the city. Told him it would take you about an hour to drive in. He said to make sure you know the city is Halloween crazy. Hey, since you have a place known for vampires already, it's going to be a Halloween heaven."

"All right. Parks. Isaac Parks," Jake said. He hung up and lowered his head. "Ashley, I'm sorry."

"Don't be—it's all right. So, this guy...the guy killed... He wasn't the nicest man in the world?"

"Apparently not. But there was a woman killed too. I mean, they may not be connected. She was a local woman, young—nothing bad that Jackson told me about, anyway. And the other... The medical examiner thinks they're associated because it looks like the same weapon was used. On one hand, I hope there aren't a lot of people running around the city with knives sharp enough to inflict that kind of damage. On the other hand... Well, I don't really know anything yet." He hesitated, looking at her. "I'm sure Jackson can get someone down here—I mean, I'll just go in to see what...what I can see."

She was strangely quiet. Then she whispered, "I dreamed of a young woman walking down Bourbon."

Jake was silent. Those who were born to the place and those who worked here were all as much family to him as they were to Ashley.

Yet, every time they came...

He was just a little bit afraid.

Yes, they saw the dead. Yes, the dead could whisper into one's mind in dreams and nightmares beyond imagination.

But he always worried about Ashley. She was honest and kind. Honorable—she did the right thing. And, he feared, that sometimes made her susceptible to those who weren't so honest and kind.

Or honorable.

She smiled. "I'm fine. I'm not being made crazy by any ghosts of Donegal Plantation. Go. I'm going to help out with the haunted house stuff here. You know, I'll go through the displays, check that no one has tried stealing a werewolf's tail, or anything of the like." He appreciated how she tried to lighten the mood. To ease his guilt at leaving her. "Go. Please, go. And keep me updated on this, okay? Louisiana, this parish, and then New Orleans... We're from here. This area is dear to our hearts." She gave him a soft kiss. "Go to work."

He sighed and rose, headed for the shower.

He was dedicated to his work. It sounded funny, but since he'd been a kid, injustice had infuriated him—he'd always wanted to be there for the victims. And now, once again, he was leaving to answer the call to help someone else. But for some reason, he stopped and turned... Even though he wasn't sure of what he'd been about to say.

Ashley sat up on the bed, sheets slightly tangled around her, her eyes on him, her hair streaming around her in a provocatively messy torrent.

He stopped and turned around, walking back to her.

She arched her brows. "'Truth, justice, and the American way' are waiting for you," she semi-quoted with a saucy grin.

"They can wait for five minutes." He kissed her just below her ear.

"A quickie?" she breathed.

"Sorry, but…"

She grinned. "I haven't a thing in the world against quickies."

And yet, neither of them really wanted quick. The passion and the fire were easy…

She clung to him, and he held her tight, not wanting to let go.

And he knew, somehow, that Jackson's phone call had changed things. As if a knock on the helm had shifted a great ship out at sea.

Maybe it had begun even before the phone had started ringing. Because Ashley hadn't even heard it all, and still…

She shoved him suddenly. "Go to work. I have ghosts and goblins and things that go bump in the night to deal with."

Real and unreal, he thought dryly.

Halloween.

What the hell had made them come at Halloween?

He had to let go of her.

Reluctantly, he did so. And hurried into the shower.

* * * *

Frazier Donegal sat tall and straight and completely dignified. He had a headful of snow-white hair, the epitome of a Southern gentleman.

Ashley kissed her grandfather's cheek as she joined him and Beth at breakfast, dressed for the day in jeans and a T-shirt.

"Why? Why do we do this? We're just flat out crazy," he said, sipping his coffee.

Ashley shook her head. "Sir, you know we do this for three reasons. A. Halloween is fun. B. We're known as a fabulous attraction—people flock here for both the re-enactment and the Halloween festivities. C. The money we make during these times helps us maintain the house, the stables, the property—and the wonderful people we are so incredibly lucky to have working here."

"Oh, yes. That's right," Frazier said and smiled proudly as he looked out the window at his property. Cliff—their horse master—was rehanging a giant spider that had slipped down a rafter.

Frazier shuddered, shook his head, and took another sip of his coffee.

"Meeting of our cast of ghoulies in thirty," Beth said, glancing at her watch. She grinned at Ashley. "We've got several new attractions this year. Wait until you see what happens at the smokehouse. You're going to love it. Honestly, we have a great group of actors this year."

"Can't wait," Ashley said. "You never hire anyone but the best."

"Of course not." Beth nodded. "Want to walk out now?"

"Sure." Ashley rose and kissed her grandfather on the top of his head. "Not to worry, sir. You can hole up in your room."

And he would, she knew. Frazier was not a fan of the plantation being turned into a haunted house. History was haunting enough, as far as he was concerned. But he did know the cogs on the giant wheel that was the plantation were expensive. And he did love his home.

More importantly, he thought it was imperative to preserve history—be it noble or ignoble. Truth and learning, in Frazier's mind, swayed the future. Lying about or hiding any event was wrong. Man could only learn through his mistakes.

"Have fun, children," he said as they headed out.

The meeting would be in the office at the stables—a really nice, big space. Years and years ago, her father had seen to it that the office was completely modernized, that the air-conditioning system was upgraded and put on a maintenance plan. There was a large desk, which had been there since 1852, a Chesterfield sofa and a number of armchairs. The stables were in mint condition as well, the horses well-tended and loved. Frazier had always had an obsession with making sure his animals received the best treatment possible.

They walked on behind the stables, though, to the smokehouse.

"Wait for it... Wait for it..." Beth said, pausing before she threw open the door with a flourish.

Ashley looked in. She tried to smile but inwardly, she winced. Through their own difficulties and Jake's work, she'd seen too much real creepiness. She knew Halloween was supposed to be fun and spooky—but the smokehouse was positively sinister this year.

Hooks that had historically held meat to feed the many mouths on the plantation now held mock human torsos and limbs. A butcher-block table was covered in blood, and a mannequin that had been partially disarticulated—as if the limbs and torso were being prepared for hanging in the smokehouse as well—lay haphazardly to the side. Blood spattered the wall, and on the ledge was a row of human heads—apparently the ones that had belonged to the mannequin bodies. They were male and female, young and old—with wide eyes and mouths open in horror.

"Whoa," Ashley said.

"Jonathan Starling is the actor who works here," Beth said. "You'll meet him in a minute. We only open Wednesday through Saturday nights—but we've been paying our actors the same as they would be getting if they were working a full-time gig. We've been voted one of the best scare attractions in the area."

"That's great."

"And we're doing very, very well financially," Beth said. Then frowned, looking at Ashley. "You okay?"

"Sure."

"It is pretty ghastly," Beth said, glancing around. "But it's what people want." She shrugged. "And it does bring in the money."

"Of course."

"Want to see the gingerbread house?"

Ashley tried to focus on the odd comment. "We have a gingerbread house?"

"Yep—just like the one from good old Hansel and Gretel."

"Um, cool."

"It's in the old kitchen... We've got time. Come on. As you know, we always do the haunted hayride thing, and we have some setups out in the old slave quarters. But I think the two features here are the scariest." She glanced over her shoulder. "Depends on what you're afraid of."

Ashley followed Beth out to the old kitchen. It had been painted in shades of beige and tan that gave the illusion it was actually made out of gingerbread. Dotted with candy around the windows, it looked completely realistic. It even smelled of gingerbread.

"We're giving out cookies on the porch at tour's end this year," Beth said. "Along with iced tea. No alcohol... A few years back, your granddad's old chum Herman from Natchez was running a haunted house and people were drinking quite a bit. One girl got scared and socked a scare actor. Poor guy ended up in the hospital. After that, your granddad says iced tea—and that's it."

"It's kind of dangerous for the scare actors, huh?" Ashley said.

"I like being the hostess on the porch," Beth said. "No danger there—other than if a cookie freak were to go crazy, but... Anyway, inside." She proudly threw open the door to the "house."

It had once been the outdoor kitchen—designed so that in case a fire should start, the kitchen could burn without the main house going down in a pile of ash as well. Donegal now had a nice, modern kitchen inside, but the old kitchen outdoors had been an integral part of the plantation in the old days, and as such was important historically and architecturally.

The hearth took up the entire back wall. There was a giant cauldron set over the center where the fire would burn.

A comfortable bed and a few chairs were set up on one side of the room.

On the other, there were…cages. Some were filled with mannequins. The others, Ashley realized, would be filled with actors.

"The wicked witch wins?" Ashley asked.

Beth laughed. "No, she's here with her sisters. Our visitors are menaced by them—from a distance. Then one is allowed to set the children free. And one lucky person gets to push Aria—the head witch—into that stove. It empties into a small shed in the back, where she screams and cackles as she bakes. The actress is Lavinia Carole. She's from Biloxi—you're going to love her. We take people in groups of twenty, so they all get their own, slightly unique, experience."

"You all have really taken it a step further this time."

"You don't mind?"

Ashley laughed. "I'm thrilled. It's all wonderful. We do the books together, so, just like you, I'm thrilled."

Beth nodded, hiding a smile. "As you know, we own most of the decorations. Just in case you want them for the wedding."

"I'll keep that in mind."

"I see that the cast of actors seems to be arriving. We can head for the stables."

"Sounds good. I have to say hello to the horses too. Nellie, Jeff, Varina, all of them. I miss them so much."

Being afraid of horses, Beth waited for her while she paid her respects. The horse master, Cliff, always saw to it that each animal was given plenty of attention, though Ashley had a special relationship with Varina, who was considered hers. But going through the stables, she showered some attention on each of the twelve horses the plantation kept.

The animals always made her feel good. They were so solid and real—and normal.

She wondered why she was so worried about *normal*.

But she knew.

The bizarre and eerie trappings on the house didn't bother her at all. Nor did the artistry of the cemetery or her family's tomb, or the tombs and graves of those who had lived and died at Donegal.

She felt haunted.

By her dream.

"Hey, time's a wasting," Beth called to her.

"Onward to the meeting," Ashley replied, and they headed to the office together.

* * * *

Jake met with Detective Parks on Broad Street.

Parks was a lean man of medium height with slightly graying hair and eyes that matched the color to a T. He shook hands with Jake, appearing genuinely glad to see him as they went to an empty conference room. Sitting down, he told Jake, "I happen to have met your Jackson Crow a few years back. Nasty business with a serial killer taking off on a ship. I was just one of a task force. Thing is, I don't think my main people wanted to call in the FBI."

Jake shrugged. Sometimes local authorities wanted federal help. Sometimes they did not.

"We try to assist local police," he said.

Parks nodded, a small smile curving his lips. "Well, we've been besieged down here over the last few years. This is my home, and God help me, the good, the bad, the crazy, I love New Orleans."

"I love the city, too."

"So I understand. You happened to be here because you're basically a local. And you're getting married, I hear. Out at Donegal Plantation."

"Yes, next month. After Halloween," Jake told him.

"Lucky man. Donegal is… It's history."

"Ashley would be happy to hear you say that," Jake said.

Then the pleasantries were over. Parks flipped open his notebook and presented a picture to Jake. "Artist's rendering of the 'witches.'"

Jake studied the drawing. There were three individuals, all exactly alike. Dressed in black, something light flowing around the more fitted costumes. The faces were green with very large noses. Whoever had created them had evidently been a fan of *The Wizard of Oz.*

"That's a bitch," Jake said, looking at Parks. "It's Halloween—the city must be crowded with characters dressed like this."

Parks nodded. Then he pulled out some photographs. "Here's what I'm not understanding. We've looked into the first victim, Shelley Broussard. She was a good kid—well, twenty-five-year-old, if that's a kid. Her parents divorced when she was young, but she made it through high school and then college and she worked in an art shop on Magazine Street. By all accounts, she was a nice person."

Jake looked at the picture of the young woman as she'd been found at the crime scene. Head bowed low. Seated cross-legged. The sign *Traitor* around her neck, and a coffee cup by her side. Money in the cup. Ironic.

Parks flipped to another picture. It was an autopsy photo. The victim lay on a steel table, a sheet resting over all but her shoulders, neck, and face.

She had been a pretty girl in life. Nicely crafted face, long, blonde hair.

"We've interviewed the people she worked with. She left the shop on Magazine last Saturday night. Her father is in the wind. Her mother remarried and lives in Texas with a passel of new kids. She hasn't been able to get here yet and, sad to say, she wasn't as horrified as a parent should be. Apparently, her new life is more important than her oldest child."

Jake nodded, not sure what to say to that. How a mother could be so enthralled with her new life that she didn't care about her daughter he couldn't comprehend. He was glad that, at least, Parks really seemed to care. And now he did too.

"Did you check her residence?"

"Yes. She lived with a few other girls in a loft above the shop where she was working."

"And?"

"And nothing. Clean as a whistle. There are two or three young women there at any given time. But, trust me, no blood. Nothing that indicated any kind of a struggle. And she was seen leaving. By several people—the owner of the shop and his wife. A few of the salesgirls."

"She's dead, and this Tink is dead. But you don't know if it's the same killer."

"That's the thing. She was a good kid. The man killed last night—

Tink, or Thomas Aldridge—had a record a mile long, including burglary and assault. He was charged with murder once, but we had to drop the charges. The D.A. didn't have enough evidence to take the case to court."

"So, one victim a sweet girl, another victim a thug. And there was an eye witness to the second murder who gave a police artist an image of three witches."

Parks nodded gravely. "I think there's something at work here. I mean…" He paused, staring at Jake. "I called Jackson Crow on purpose, rather than trying to reach someone in the main behavioral science units. Some of the guys here scoff at the BAU to begin with, but you already know that."

"I know many officers don't believe in profiling, yes. And I know many call us the ghost busters."

"But you always get your man. Or woman. Or both. Or… Well, you have a solve record that's incredible. Thing is, Special Agent Mallory, I know you've been with Crow since the beginning—when your unit had six members and you started out solving that case in the Quarter. And I know about the murders at Donegal. And I know, too, this is just the beginning. These witches are going to terrorize NOLA. At Halloween." He sighed. "I need your help."

"Sir, you've got it." Jake sat back. "I'd like to see your eye witness. Then I'd like to interview Shelley Broussard's friends at the art shop myself."

"The first you can do right now. I've asked that David Henderson be brought to a conference room."

"Jackson mentioned you're holding him in jail."

"He's terrified. Won't go home. I've arranged to detain him for a few days, pending charges. He'll admit to having done anything right now—he doesn't want to go back out on the streets. Not until Halloween is over, at least. And then again, maybe never. He thinks," Parks added, "the prison guards will be able to stop the witches before they can get to him."

Other officers greeted Parks respectfully and looked curiously at Jake as they walked down the hallway to the interview room. The officer guarding the door nodded and opened it for them.

David Henderson sat at a table, twitching nervously, staring down at his lap. There were two chairs across from him and his head jerked up as Jake and Parks took them, even though he hadn't moved when they'd entered the room.

"This is Special Agent Mallory. He's from the area, David. He's going to help us look into the murder of Tink. I need you to tell him everything that you've told me."

"Witches man, they're real," David Henderson said. He was probably in his mid-thirties, and appeared haggard—like a man who wasn't in withdrawal, but one who did spend at least some time with recreational drugs. He stopped twitching as he looked at Jake, but began nervously working his hands. He wasn't cuffed, but then again, he wasn't really under arrest. Yet.

Jake nodded. "Could you give me some more detail?"

"I admit it—we were meeting to rob a house. You gotta understand Tink. He was mammoth. You're a big guy, Mr. Special Agent, but Tink... He was huge. He could scare anyone. And when he walked up to those witches, they knew... They knew he was about to belt one of them, and... The lead one, she stepped out. I never saw what she hit him with, but...he turned. And it was like a frickin' geyser, man. Blood everywhere. She just slashed him...so hard and so fast. And he was down."

"They were all alike? All three of them?" Jake asked.

Henderson nodded. "Noses, man, they had big noses."

"But height, size?" Jake pressed.

That produced a pause. "No... The main one, she was taller. I mean, I was at a distance, but... Yeah. The one on her left was heavier, and maybe a few inches shorter. And the other one was shorter than that...and skinny, I think. But they were all witches. Wiccans, or whatever."

"Wicca is actually a religion, and real wiccans believe in doing no harm," Jake said. "Halloween witches—let's go with that."

But Henderson shook his head. "No, man, they were real. You look at them, and you know—they were real. Okay, so they weren't Wicca people, or whatever that is. Maybe they were voodoo witches. This is New Orleans."

"Voodoo is a religion, too. No human sacrifices on the street," Jake told him, trying to be patient. "Not from people really practicing."

"Hey, man, you a voodoo priest or a witch yourself?" Henderson asked.

"No."

"Vampire?"

"No."

The man was clearly terrified. Truly convinced there were real witches at work in the city of New Orleans.

"David, these were people dressed up. In really good makeup and costumes, I'd guess. Did you see the weapon they used?"

He shook his head. "I'll bet she used a fingernail. Don't witches have mile-long nails?"

"No fingernail made a clean gash like that on a man's throat," Detective Parks said quietly.

"Maybe she keeps a blade attached to it," Henderson suggested.

"Where did they go after Tink—dropped?" Jake asked.

"I don't know. I ran—I ran like hell. I ran to Frenchmen Street where there were people. I found a cop. After that... I don't know."

"Okay. Thank you, David," Jake said.

The man looked at Parks with anguish in his eyes. "You're not going to throw me out on the street now, are you?"

"No, David," Parks assured him.

When they were out of the room, Parks asked Jake, "Do you need to see the bodies?"

"Maybe. But right now I want to visit that shop on Magazine Street."

Parks nodded gravely. "Her coworkers were her closest friends, I think. She was something of an artist herself. I saw some of her work. She might have been really good in time."

Parks actually seemed sad. Detectives had to learn not to take death to heart. But maybe, this time, Parks just hadn't been able to manage it.

"Do you have a plan after you go to the shop?" Parks asked.

"Yep."

"What's that?"

"A lot of walking—through the Quarter and beyond."

* * * *

Lavinia Carole was an attractive, lithe young woman with pink and blue streaks in her short brown hair. She was happy to meet Ashley and quick to tell her how much she was loving the job at Donegal.

Beth next introduced Ashley to Jonathan Starling—the man who worked in the smokehouse. Appearing to be in his late twenties, he was about six-feet tall and built, but not muscle-ᵇ

"You thought I'd be bigger, eh?" he teased aι "I make up for it with my menacing grin."

Ashley laughed. "You're not small, my friend."

"Just not a giant," he said.

Next she met Artie Lane, Trina DeMoine, H.   ⌐orn, and Sandy Patterson, the "ghosts" who appeared on the haunted hayride. Then Alex Maple, Bill Davis, and Jerry Harte, costumed actors who led the groups around. And then Valerie Deering and Rhonda Blackstone, the "sister witches" who worked with Lavinia Carole.

"We have another ten people on payroll for this," Beth told her. "They aren't in costume—they're from Garrison Event Security— we've worked with them every year."

"Yes, I remember. They're great." And they were. The company did background checks on their people and hired only those who knew how to handle crowd management. They escorted out anyone creating problems, and ushered people along the right way. There were also two cops on duty at the plantation every time they held such an event.

"So," Beth said. "Get comfortable. Halloween occurs next Tuesday. That will be our last night, but it will be a big night, as you all can imagine."

"I came here last Halloween as an attendee," Lavinia said. "It was great—but working here is even better."

The others agreed. Echoes went around the room—they were all new actors this year, but it seemed several had attended in the past. Ashley hadn't met any of them before, but then, when she had been here for the event, she'd been busy. Faces became a blur.

"We'd like to know if anything is bothering any of you, if there are any trouble spots. If there's anything you may need or think we might handle better," Beth said.

"I had a bit of a problem the other night," Rhonda Blackstone said. She, like Lavinia Carole, seemed to be in her mid- to late-twenties. She was thin and blonde, not particularly beautiful, but cute and energetic.

"What happened?" Ashley asked. She'd meant to keep silent because Beth managed this, but she was curious. And Beth would have asked the same question.

"A kid kept trying to grab at me," Rhonda said. "He was obnoxious."

"Okay. Next time, motion to the security man or woman who's assigned to be with you," Beth said.

"We keep the rules posted," Ashley added. "The actors won't touch the visitors, and the visitors aren't allowed to touch the actors. We have that in every advertisement that goes out—and posted on the porch. Beth is right—we hate to be mean, but if anyone goes after you, we state clearly we have the right to escort them out."

"That's good," Valerie Deering said. "Rhonda's guy was about thirteen—a snot-nosed kid. I had an older man who kept asking me if I wanted to stir up something of a witch's brew with him later. And I swear he was trying to cop a feel."

"Don't let me see this guy," Jonathan said. "Sorry," he added quickly. "I wouldn't bash him or anything—I'd just see he was put outside the Donegal gates right fast."

"That's why we hire security," Ashley assured him.

"I didn't want to cause trouble," Rhonda said hastily.

"Nor me," Valerie added.

"You won't be causing trouble. And trust me," Ashley said, "we want Halloween to go smoothly for everyone. You all included."

Beth glanced at her notes. "I also wanted to assure you there will still be no more than twenty in each group through the kitchen and the smokehouse. Ghosts—don't you take any guff from anyone either, all right?"

Trina laughed. She was older than the others—possibly forty or so. She appeared to be the athletic type, wiry and fit, with short blonde hair and sparkling green eyes.

"We ghosts keep our distance," she assured Ashley. "Four- to six-feet from the hay wagon at all times. We haven't had any trouble, and we're not expecting any on Halloween either. We're careful. Your grandfather gave us a speech about how he doesn't want any of us hurt." She hesitated. "He also told us we have to stay a good fifty feet away from the cemetery at all times. That's cool. Though it would be fun to come from that direction."

She said the last with hope.

"Sorry. My grandfather is too respectful of the dead, I'm afraid. I can't change that ruling," Ashley told her.

"People don't mess with me or Harold," Artie said. "I'm the ghost who walks around with an ax in my head and Harold has a pirate sword. They see us and shrink into each other on the wagon. Hey, what's the rule with costumes this year?"

"No costumes for the visitors, only the actors. We offer them a place to dress up after, if they want," Beth said. "It will be no different on Halloween."

There were a few more general questions, and then the meeting broke.

Lavinia Carole lingered a moment, pausing to ask Ashley if she would be there that night.

"I—" She started to say yes, but didn't get the chance.

Her phone rang. And she saw that it was Jake.

"Excuse me," she murmured, and turned away to answer it.

"Dinner?" Jake asked her.

She frowned. "Yes, we usually do eat it."

"In the Quarter. With me."

"Romantic—or on the case?"

"Unfortunately, on the case. But we'll still have a nice dinner. I promise."

"Sure. Are you driving back for me, or…?"

"Can you come in? Get a lift if you can. We'll only have one car that way."

"Okay."

"And one more thing."

"What?"

"If you see a trio of witches, get the hell away."

"Funny."

"No. Not funny. Promise, if you should see witches, get the hell away."

"Okay. I promise."

She looked up. Lavinia Carole was waiting politely for her answer.

Well, at least she was no longer with a "trio" of witches.

She was with just one.

She smiled, shaking her head mentally. Donegal Plantation witches could have nothing to do with other witches.

"Lavinia, I won't make it tonight. But I will be here tomorrow."

"Oh, good. I hope you'll like what we do."

"I'm sure I will," Ashley said. "I hear the good guys always win."

Chapter 3

Heading toward Magazine Street and searching for a place to park, Jake wondered at his wisdom in asking Ashley to join him in the Quarter. He should have wandered the streets alone. But he wasn't sure what he expected. He didn't think the three killer "witches" would be calmly walking down Bourbon Street. They had to know they'd been witnessed.

Then again, there were costume parties going on all over the city this week. Halloween would fall on Tuesday—and it was Wednesday now.

Just six days to go.

What was frightening was the fact the body count could rise in those few days. People blithely walking around, in and out of costume, thinking nothing of seeing witches. Parks had told him they were putting out a newscast so people would be on the lookout. But...

It was Halloween.

Which witch was which?

He found parking and looked down the street. Shops were outfitted for the season. Spiders, ghosts, goblins—and witches—were set in window displays.

They were everywhere.

He found the art shop—"Picture This"—right next to one of his favorite donut shops. A little bell tinkled over his head as he entered.

Inside, he found a good-sized showroom with a few fake walls set up to allow more space for paintings.

He saw many of the usual images found in this kind of NOLA shop—artists' visions of Jackson Square, the Cathedral, Bourbon Street, the river... Steamboats, musicians on the street. Day-to-day life in the Big Easy. Some renderings were realistic, some had a touch of fantasy.

There were other paintings as well. One wall, dedicated to Halloween, had a painting of a laughing bevy of ghosts. Another showed the torment in a man's eyes as he went from being a man to a werewolf. Another showed a beautiful witch in a pointed hat, staring sadly at the moon as if she, too, would turn into something evil once it rose higher in the night sky.

"Hello?"

A woman came from a doorway in the back—there was an office to the rear, Jake assumed.

She was middle-aged, of medium height, with short, curly red hair and a pleasant manner. She wore jeans and an attractive tailored shirt and jacket.

"Welcome." She smiled. "May I help you? All of our work is done by local artists. Yes, sometimes you can find them working down at Jackson Square. But we love having a real home for our local talent, and this is it."

"Nice," Jake said, offering his hand. "I have to admit right off that I'm afraid I'm not here to shop. I've come to ask you about Shelley Broussard."

"Oh," she said softly. Her eyes appeared to water and her smile faded. "Shelley," she whispered, turning toward the door as if the girl might be coming through it at any moment.

"I'm sorry to cause you distress. But we're determined to find her killer." He produced his badge and credentials. "Jake Mallory, ma'am. I understand she left work here, and that's the last time she was seen."

The woman nodded.

"Are you the owner?" he asked.

She nodded again. "Myself and my husband, Nick. I'm Marty—Marty Nicholson. We—we loved Shelley. That's some of her work over there. Her mother hasn't come and we're thinking we may need funds for her funeral. She'll be buried up in the Garden District. She loved Lafayette Cemetery. She has some family there so she'll go in with them."

"I'm so sorry," Jake said. "Can I ask you some questions? Detective Parks believed her closest friends were here."

"Yes. My husband and I… We were very fond of her. And our other girls as well. They were all best friends."

"Your other girls?"

"Samantha and Emily. We met Shelley on Jackson Square. We're not local—not originally. We're from Texas. Anyway, Nick saw Shelley's work one day when we were just out walking in the Quarter. She had such talent. Nick was very taken with her paintings from the get-go—and she was asking practically nothing for them. So, Nick being the good businessman he is, conceived the idea of the store here. He found the place to rent and got it up and going in less than a week. We found some other locals who were working for a fraction of what they were worth—and we offered them a venue. Each artist works in the store a few hours per week."

"That was very kind of you and your husband."

"I told you he's a good businessman," she said dryly. "We're doing quite well."

"That's great to hear. Can you tell me anything about the day Shelley was last seen?"

"It was like any other day. She and Samantha Perkins were working the floor. Oh, Emily Dupont was here as well—she had just brought in that gorgeous painting of the riverboat over there. They were laughing together, and talking about meeting up that night. It's ironic—Nick was telling them all to be careful. We've had a rash of crime going on."

Jake nodded but didn't interrupt her train of thought.

"They were going to meet at Lafitte's." She paused, swallowing. "Emily and Samantha went out as planned, but Shelley didn't show. It was the next day—Sunday—when they...when they found her."

"You saw her leave the shop?"

"Yes. She headed out and down the street. She was on foot. Shelley didn't have a car."

"If she had just gotten off work, why didn't she go up to her room?"

"She had shopping to do, she told us. She wanted to buy a costume for Halloween. There are all kinds of balls in the city. One that honors Anne Rice. One that's just huge and run by a guy who does vampire balls all over the world. And more—and more and more—every year."

"She just left, walking down Magazine. And none of you saw her again?"

"No," she whispered.

"May I see her room?"

"Sure."

Marty Nicholson locked the front door and switched the *Open* sign to *Closed*.

She led him into the back, where there were canvases and easels, rows of paints and brushes and other paraphernalia.

"Stairs are here. And right in back, there's a set that leads down to the street too."

"Kind of you to give the girls a place to live."

"Kind—and good business," Marty said. "This way, there's most often someone on the property. We have an alarm system, but if people know someone is almost always here, that will deter most petty crooks."

"Good thinking."

He followed her up the stairway. At the top was a small landing. There were three doors, all of them open. One was to a bathroom, one to a compact kitchen, and one to a dorm-like room.

No one was present.

The dorm room offered three beds, each with a nightstand by it. There was a closet and a large dresser. The drawers were labeled *Emily*, *Samantha*, and *Shelley*.

"I haven't had the heart to clear out her things yet," Marty murmured. "I need to do that."

Jake walked over to Shelley's bed first. He sat for a minute and waited, trying to sense Shelley, get a feel of her spirit.

Trying to see if, perhaps, it lingered.

He opened the drawer on her nightstand. There were phone chargers, pens, little sample perfumes, and a paperweight with the NOLA fleur-de-lis.

And a notebook.

He picked it up and flipped it open.

The first page was filled with enthusiasm about a new project. A painting of the Cathedral.

The second page talked about a boy she had met—she'd been crazy about him. He'd had to return to school in Philadelphia.

The third page...

Had only one sentence.

I believe...but what is right is right, and what is wrong...is very wrong.

The rest of the notebook was empty. He set it back in the drawer.

As he did so, he saw something he'd missed at first glance. A crucifix. Gold and intricately worked.

"Beautiful," he noted. "I'm surprised she wasn't wearing this."

"Oh, well... She was a free-thinker. Maybe she thought it was wrong to wear. She had compassion for everyone. She might have thought the church was too hard on sinners or something—I don't really know."

"I guess you'll see that her mother gets it."

The mother who hadn't bothered to come get her.

"Yes, I suppose. I intend to box everything up. I'll offer it to her mother—if she ever arrives. And if not... Emily and Samantha were her best friends."

Jake rose. "Did she have any enemies? Any disputes—no matter how small—with anyone?"

"Good Lord, no. She was amazing. People loved her. Except—" She paused. "Oh, maybe it's nothing."

"What, please?"

"There was a young man. A really good-looking young man. He was in the shop several times. I know he had a thing for her. And she seemed to like him too, but... I think he came on a little strong. Nothing violent ever happened. I just heard her telling him one day she didn't know. And he left in a bit of a huff."

"What was his name?"

"I'm not sure. Maybe Emily or Samantha could tell you."

"Where can I find them?"

"They're both off, but they might be working at Jackson Square. I'll get you their cell phone numbers. If you're finished here?"

"A moment," Jake said.

He opened Shelley's dresser drawer. Nothing but jeans, leggings, T-shirts, and a few nice blouses.

He went into the closet. Labels there hung above the neatly arranged clothing.

Shelley Broussard had one long coat, a few jackets, and a few tailored shirts.

He checked the pockets. Nothing.

"Finished here," he told Marty.

"Come on down," she said.

In the storeroom below she paused at a desk, got paper, and looked in an appointment book, flipping to an address page. She wrote down numbers for him.

"Come anytime, Mr. Mallory. Um, Agent Mallory?"

"Jake. Call me Jake, ma'am. That will do. And yes, I'm sorry to distress you, but I probably will be back."

He headed on out.

Right now, Jackson Square seemed the place to be.

* * * *

The wedding was set for Saturday, November 11. Luckily, many of the Krewe members were couples—maybe because they were some of the only people who might really understand one another and truly be able to share their lives. It would be easy to fit them into the main house and into some of the other outbuildings on the property. Donegal had never been burned, and many of the slave quarters remained. Frazier's father had been the one to see that a sign above each read *Lest We Forget*.

Ashley had spent several hours talking about the wedding with her grandfather and Beth. Frazier was so excited—he'd been giving them very strong hints about marriage for a long time now. "I finally get to walk you down the staircase. And bless the saints, I'm not getting any younger, you know."

"I'll see that you make it to a hundred," she promised.

But after they'd spoken, she was restless. Beth really had the whole "haunted plantation" going smoothly and Ashley didn't want to interfere.

She thought about taking her horse out for a ride, but decided what she really wanted to do was go ahead and get to the city. Beth offered to drive her but she decided on Uber. It was an hour's drive, and she felt a little guilty at the cost, but when her Uber driver arrived, he was enthusiastic—fare in, and fare out. It was a nice little piece of change for him.

She decided to treat herself to a late lunch in the Garden District at Commander's Palace. Then she roamed Lafayette Cemetery for a few minutes, marveling at the beauty that had been given over to the dead. A stop in a Garden District bookstore enthralled her for nearly an hour. She made a purchase—a new book on the history of Orleans Parish—and then called another Uber and headed for Jackson Square.

Once there, she just walked around. Palm readers and spiritualists of all kinds were busy in front of the Cathedral.

And all around, musicians were playing.

Artists were hard at work, displaying their paintings and sketches and doing caricatures. She wandered, admiring a great deal of it, and then she paused, really loving a painting of the equestrian statue of Andrew Jackson that stood in the center of the square.

She saw that the artist—a woman in her early thirties, brown hair bound back in a bandana—was watching her.

"Stunning," Ashley said.

"Thank you. I love the statue. I love... Well, I love everything here. I love New Orleans."

Ashley smiled. "You're not from here?"

"New York City. Can't you tell?" The woman grinned.

Ashley laughed. "Ask me if I want a cup of coffee—that will let me know. Seriously, no, I didn't. You don't have much of an accent."

"I'm from Manhattan. I guess the accents are mainly the Bronx and Brooklyn. Maybe Queens. Anyway, I came down here, and that was it. I'm home. I love this place. You're local?"

"From about an hour away," Ashley said. "And I understand. I love the city, too. I love the old architecture. The music. The Cathedral and the buildings surrounding that magnificent statue of Jackson. The mule-drawn carriages, and the river and... Well, everything."

A number of people were looking at the woman's paintings so Ashley excused herself. She studied another piece, one that pictured buskers playing on Royal Street by the Omni Hotel. A crowd gathered while others walked by. The painting appeared to almost come to life.

"Oh, yes. Yes," Ashley heard the woman say, and turned.

She was talking to a man who had walked up. He was probably close to fifty, but his age fit him well. He was tall and lean, with graying hair and a truly handsome, charismatic face.

He looked up and saw Ashley watching him. He smiled and she was surprised to feel a small sense of trembling. Of unease, almost.

She smiled in return and he walked over to her.

"Are you an artist, miss?"

"No, I'm afraid not. I'm a tour guide in Alexandria."

"Well, if not an artist, you could certainly be an artist's model. And if you like art, you must come by my place." He produced a card and handed it to her. The card was well done, with pale images of the very area where they stood backing up the words. *Picture This—Nick and Marty Nicholson, owners and operators.*

"It's on Magazine Street. Oh, are you familiar with the area?"

"Yes, I know Magazine Street," she said.

"Come by. Miss Gerry here will now be displaying with us. We do our best to find the most amazing local talent—and then give them all a showcase. We... We've recently had a loss and we think that Gerry will fill it well."

"That's lovely. I will stop by," Ashley said.

"Do," he said softly. "And good day to you."

If he'd been wearing a hat, he would have tipped it, Ashley thought. But he merely smiled and inclined his head, and then turned around and headed toward Chartres Street.

"Wow," the woman he'd called Gerry said.

"Wow is right," Ashley told her.

"Seriously, being asked to be a member of his shop... That's huge. He gives you a place to live and everything. All I have to do is work at the shop for a few days each week. I'm so lucky."

"That's great. Absolutely great. Congratulations."

The woman offered her hand. "Gerry. Or Geraldine. Sands. Gerry Sands. My signature on my paintings is hard to read. I can draw and paint, but go figure—my cursive is terrible. If you'd like that painting, I believe it will cost a great deal more once I'm moved over into the shop." She laughed.

"I do love the painting and I want to buy it. I don't have a car at the moment, though."

"I'll hold it for you. At the price on it now."

"Done deal." Ashley wrote out a check, deciding not to explain why it listed a Virginia address when she'd just said she was from the area. Thankfully, Gerry didn't seem to notice.

Leaving the artist—and her newly purchased painting—Ashley continued her journey around the square. She realized now that many of the paintings being displayed were in honor of Halloween. Some were truly creepy.

Many were of witches.

When she left Jackson Square and crossed Chartres on her way up to Royal, she passed a number of places where Halloween was—just like at Donegal Plantation—out in full scale.

Ghosts.

Goblins.

Creatures.

Witches.

Here, there, and everywhere.

Watch out for witches.

Yep. Great advice. At Halloween.

She gave herself a mental shake at the sarcasm and hurried on to one of her favorite shops—Fifi Mahony's—where she loved to browse the fantastic wigs created there and sometimes have her hair done in the salon.

She was due to meet Jake in an hour.

Witches.

She passed more and more of them. They were pictured in decals, in hanging decorations, and by mannequins in the front of shops.

Witches. Yes, here, there, and everywhere.

But, at least, no trio of witches.

She hurried up the steps and into Fifi Mahony's.

Chapter 4

Jake walked down Magazine Street and watched the blur of activities. Halloween was still six days away and it was a Wednesday night, but the city was in full party mode. Some just walked the streets—locals who were weary of Halloween starting early, visitors totally into the mood, and those who were local and just loved Halloween.

People did love Halloween. It was early and he already saw couples with children dressed as ninjas, Star Wars characters, and more.

There were a few mummies and ghouls and the like walking the streets—one in particular delighted a number of children, stopping to make a howling noise, and then pretending to cry when they jumped back. People laughed. It was all in good fun.

He was surprised when the ghoul walked up to him. "Jake? Jake Mallory?"

Jake stared at the creature.

"Football, man. It's Sammy Riley. We played together in high school—I was one of your linebackers."

"Hey. How are you, Sammy?"

"Good. Having a little fun with the kids. I'm doing a party tonight—Swamp Creatures. What are you doing here? Someone told me that you're a Fed now."

"I am, and you?"

"I'm a contractor—and a scare actor at Halloween. Love it—I have so much fun."

"I saw that. Great."

"You should come to the party."

"Don't have an invite or a ticket."

"You don't need one. It's put on by a group of artists and musicians and even writers in the city. A really cool rich dude who got a bunch of movies made from his stuff—on the science fiction channels—pays the groundwork and the venue. No open bar, but you should come. It's in a warehouse between the CBD and the Irish Channel."

"Sounds good, but I'm meeting up with my fiancée, Ashley."

"Bring her. Oh, my God, of course, Ashley. Ashley Donegal."

"Yes, that's her. We were really just going to have dinner."

"I guess Donegal Plantation is crazy enough. Still, man… We're having all kinds of cool stuff. And these people really get into it. Vampires, werewolves, aliens, witches, you name it." He broke off, his eyes going wide. "Have you seen the news? Maybe there won't be any witches. I mean, people won't want a witch association right now, huh? Oh, hey, man, are you here because of the news?"

"I know about it," Jake said. "And, naturally, it's a crime, and I am a Fed…"

"Maybe you should come. What if there are witches there?" Sammy asked. He looked different with white makeup enhanced by shades of red and black covering his face and bandages wrapped around his body.

"No costumes, I'm afraid," Jake said.

"There's a place just down the block that rents them," Sammy told him.

"Well, maybe later. We're going to have dinner at Antoine's. Then, we'll see. We just show up?"

"Get to the door and use my name. They'll bring you right in. Do come. It's great to see you. It's been too long."

"Great to see you, too."

Sammy started to walk on, but then he hesitated. "How long you been here? I mean, did you know about the witches? Do the Feds come in when it has to do with kidnapping, state lines, and witches?"

"We actually came to plan the wedding, Sammy. You'll be invited."

"At Donegal Plantation?"

"Yep."

"Ah, man, I'll be there."

Sammy waved and continued on his way. Jake hurried to the car, pulling out his phone as he went. A feeling of fear registered in his gut and he suddenly wished he hadn't urged Ashley to come into the city.

It made no sense. One victim, sweet, talented, and beloved. Another, a dangerous hood.

Ashley was bright, smart as a whip. Through the years, when she'd been in meetings or just working with some of the agents one on one, she'd had an insight the rest of them hadn't fathomed.

She'd be fine. She was smart. She was prepared.

But he began to worry. She'd also had a dream, a nightmare. It was being back at Donegal.

Memories were popping up.

They'd visited Donegal before. But this was...

He dialed her number.

"Hey, Jake," Ashley answered with her normal enthusiasm. He decided to bury his fears. For now.

"Antoine's? That's romantic, right?" It took everything in him not to beg her to stay at the plantation.

"Antoine's would be great. See you there."

He heard the background noise and realized she must already be in the Quarter. "Where are you?"

"Just leaving Fifi Mahony's. I ordered some new wigs for the next re-enactment and met up with some old friends."

"Nice. Okay. Well, the streets are a little crazy."

"A little? Yes. Actually, the streets are always a little crazy."

"Crazier."

"I'm fine, Jake. See you there."

Ashley rang off.

She was fine, Jake told himself.

Witches...

Like Sammy had said, the witches just might not be out. They knew they'd been seen.

Which just meant that they'd be dressed up as something else. And he wanted to stay in the city to see what he could see.

It was a big city. If there were witches about...

They might plan on attending a big party.

* * * *

Ashley loved a number of the restaurants in the French Quarter and surrounding area, but Antoine's had always been a favorite. Her parents had brought her here when she'd been a child after she'd seen the movie *Dinner at Antoine's*. The memory was a good one, and coming back always reminded her of them in the best way.

She sat at the bar with a soda while she waited for Jake. It seemed as if she shouldn't imbibe, but she wasn't sure why. Except that she didn't want any dreams or visions that weren't...

Real?

Fueled by alcohol?

She pulled out her phone to check the news—and to see if she could discover what the whole thing about witches was.

The first thing to pop up on her screen quickly told her.

She read about the murder of the young artist Shelley Broussard, and then about the man who had seen his friend—a man with a record—murdered by witches.

It wasn't that New Orleans was crime-free. It was a big city and had never been immune to violence. But she hated to see what had happened. Hated that a beautiful young woman had been murdered.

Hated that it had happened around Halloween.

And by witches.

"This seat taken?"

She turned and smiled. Jake was there, looking exceptionally handsome in a casual jacket and trousers. No tie, shirt slightly open. He was very tall—six-four—and his shoulders were nicely broad, but he could appear almost lean. His hair was at a rakish angle over his forehead.

"I'll make room for you, sir," she said.

"Soda?"

"Yes. With lime. Makes it fancy."

He ordered for them both and took her hand, twining their fingers. "Should be champagne."

"Not tonight."

"No, not tonight," he agreed. "But, I promise..."

She heard the guilt in his voice and tightened her grip, willing him to understand. "Jake, it's all right. I promise. This isn't just what you do—it's who you are. And, I'm proud of that."

"You're doing okay, right?"

"Of course. Oh, because I was dreaming."

"I really don't like what's going on."

"With me—or the murdered girl and the slashed hood?"

"All of the above," he sighed. "But for now, let's focus on dinner."

"What did you do? You think these are associated? Tell me—"

"After." He brushed her lips with his. "Let's have an almost romantic dinner first."

The *maître'd* showed them to their table. Ashley loved the sense of history at Antoine's. And the food was amazing too.

Once they were seated and had ordered, Jake smiled. "Wedding plans. How are they going?"

"The space is all cleared out for the wedding. We have plenty of room—luckily, a lot of our friends come as couples, so doubling them up won't be a problem. No rooms are rented out for the weeks before and after. Oh, and you know how the main hall has the winding staircases on either side? I'll come down the left with Frazier. He's so excited. We'll be married at the base of the stairs, and then take the reception out to the grounds. It really should be beautiful. Actually, whatever we do will be beautiful. You know, I'd be fine with a justice of the peace."

"I would never do that to your grandfather," he chuckled.

"No, I guess not." She grinned.

He leaned toward her, twirling soda in his glass. "So, do you have plans for later?"

"I always have plans." She loved that she could be playful with him.

"You really are beautiful, my love."

"Thank you." She touched his hand. "You're not too shabby yourself."

"Think I have a chance of getting lucky tonight?"

"Keep up the good lines."

They were leaning close over the glittering place servings and snowy white tablecloth.

"I might just seduce you, handsome. If you play it right."

"Hm. Let's see… In a movie, this scenario might lead to you slipping off something silky you're wearing and teasing me with it…"

"Oh?" Ashley set her hand on his knee.

"Um."

"Like this?" She winked at him.

He stared at her, seemingly shocked, as she slid a piece of fabric over his lap.

"Ashley..." His face had gone a wonderful shade of red.

"Sorry, stud. It's just a napkin."

He laughed. "Okay, okay."

"I want to hear about today."

He took a breath as they both sat back in their chairs. And then he told her. First he told her about his meeting with Isaac Parks, and then his time at the store. He even mentioned running into Sammy.

"So we're going to a party?" she asked.

"I don't know. I shouldn't have had you come in."

"Yes, you should have. There will be security at the party—you know that. And we can rent costumes. Let's do it."

"Ashley, from what I understand," he said very seriously, "these killers slash so fast there's no time to react."

"But we're forewarned. And I'm with you. And you're an armed federal agent."

He still hesitated.

Ashley suddenly sat up straight.

"What?" Jake was instantly on alert.

"What was the name of that art shop?"

"Picture This."

"Really? I met the man who owns it."

"You did? I met the wife. Were you on Magazine? Ashley, where did you see him? Nick. Nick Nicholson, right?"

She nodded, digging into her bag and handing him the card the man had given her. "I fell in love with some paintings by an artist on Jackson Square. While I was admiring her work, some other customers came up. And then I heard her talking to someone. I looked at him and he was looking at me. He wanted to know if I was an artist, too. I told him no, and he gave me the card and asked me to stop by. Then, when he was gone, the artist I liked told me that he'd asked her to come show with him. But they don't just show..."

"Right. The artists work in the shop a few days a week. And the Nicholsons, naturally, take a percentage of all sales."

"Yes. But the artists get—"

"Free room and board."

"Jake—"

"I think they need to bear a much heavier scrutiny."

"Because?"

"Because Shelley Broussard was living there when she was

murdered. Because that shop was the last place she was seen alive. She—she isn't even in the ground and they're busy giving her room away."

"They might just be good people."

"Sure," Jake conceded. "They might—and they might not."

"He was strange," Ashley said.

"How so?"

"I don't know. He's a handsome man, dignified looking, but there was something about him…"

"Did he look like a witch?"

"No. Not at all. Like a corporate bigwig, the kind who could charm you into giving him your savings for a hedge fund. What about her?"

"Very… normal. But…"

"But what?"

He sat back. "I tried to reach the other two girls living there currently, Emily and Samantha. They didn't answer their cell phones, but I left messages. Neither called me back." He drummed his fingers on the table.

"Maybe they were busy. Artists, right? Maybe they were painting."

"Maybe."

Jake was thoughtful. And Ashley understood. She didn't want to explain why she'd had an odd feeling about Mr. Nicholson. Because Jake—being Jake—would worry about her. And that was the last thing he needed on his mind right now.

Finally he shook his head. "Apparently, they're set up to house three young women at one time. There's a room upstairs with three beds. I went through the drawer in Shelley Broussard's nightstand. She left a notebook and she had written something about right being right and wrong being wrong. I have the exact words in my notes. At least, I think they're the exact words. I waited until I got to the car—I didn't want it to appear like anything really interested me. Unless I have something solid, I need people to keep welcoming me. Shelley Broussard has a mother living in Texas, but according to Parks, she hasn't even been that interested in coming for her daughter's remains."

"Wow." Ashley couldn't imagine a mother being that uninterested.

"I know." Several emotions played over his face.

"The notebook bothered you?"

"Yes. It was as if she was sticking to her guns about something. And when she was found, she had a sign on her that read *Traitor*. But that's not all. There was a crucifix in her drawer. A really beautiful gold crucifix. It bothered me that she would have such a piece and not be wearing it."

"People don't always wear their jewelry."

But Jake still seemed disturbed. "I don't know. I just don't know. Unless she was changing something about her life. She might have been raised Catholic, and then when her mother remarried she changed? It doesn't seem right. I don't know, but—" He seemed to shake off his thoughts. "Let's focus on something a little lighter for now. We can rent costumes in a store that's near the art shop, right?"

"Let's do it." She smiled at him. "We'll skip dessert. Champagne and *crème brûlée* next time around."

"Ashley," Jake murmured.

"Jake," she countered, knowing he was concerned for her safety. "It's ridiculous—for one—to assume these murderers are going to a particular party. You did intend to just walk around and watch what was going on, right? Hoping you'd pick up on some kind of clue."

"Yes."

"Stop worrying. And when we're home… Well, maybe something silk can really fall your way. Or mine." She smiled. "Remember when we tried the silk sheets?"

"Yes. We wound up on the floor. Actually, even that—"

"We did have a few bruises. Anyway, stud, that's for later." She motioned for the check.

They were going to a party.

"Ashley…" He tried one more time.

"Jake, I'm in this with you. I've always been in this with you. And we're in New Orleans. Orleans Parish. We're home. Have faith in me. Don't just love me, have faith in me."

"I do," he swore softly.

Jake looked at her, his eyes serious. "I don't know how I could survive—function—if I didn't have you."

She reached across the table and took his hand. "It's going to be fine."

His expression told her he wasn't so sure. "We'll get through it. Together."

Chapter 5

"So that's it," Ashley said, facing the façade of "Picture This."

It was like any other art shop. The large picture windows featured some of the best of what was to be found inside. An *Open* sign was in the front door.

They had left the French Quarter behind for the wonders of Magazine Street, which was lined with more restaurants, clubs, and shops, many of these the favorite haunts of locals.

The costume shop was still down the street. But the art shop fascinated Ashley. And Jake hadn't yet reached the other two girls—Emily Dupont and Samantha Perkins.

One—or both of them—might be working now.

"I say we go in," she added.

Jake looked at her uneasily. "Maybe you shouldn't be associated with me."

"Ah, but maybe I should be."

Ashley didn't give him a chance to protest. She opened the door. A bell tinkled as she did so.

There were others in the shop. An attractive brunette of about thirty was helping a couple who were enamored with a painting of Royal Street. The picture captured the beautiful Hotel Monteleone and a group of musicians playing just across the street, all facing the neon lights of Canal Street.

Ashley began to wander, and Jake followed close behind.

"These are beautiful—and interesting," Ashley said, pausing before a group of paintings.

They were odd. One was of a werewolf—tortured as he changed from man to beast.

Another showed a witch—not a cackling, big-nosed witch, but a lovely young witch with huge round eyes. She was staring up at the moon with fear. The painting was both beautiful and somehow tragic.

"They were created by our victim," Jake said softly. "Shelley Broussard."

"It's as if her mind was…tortured."

"Maybe she knew she didn't have much time left," Jake murmured. "Maybe her paintings were a cry for help."

"Yes. And maybe a way to…to lead people to her killer." Ashley turned. "She was afraid, Jake. She was afraid of exactly what happened to her. She did something—or maybe didn't do something? But what was it exactly?"

Jake had reviewed his notes in the car so he didn't need to look at them now. In fact, he'd memorized the words.

"I believe…but what is right is right, and what is wrong…is very wrong."

"It sounds as if she was having a crisis of faith—or maybe heart? Something."

"Possibly." Jake shrugged. "Tomorrow I'm going to reach that girl's mother—the one who can't quite get herself to leave Texas to claim her daughter's body." He shook his head.

The thirtyish brunette came over to them wearing a big smile. "Hello, welcome. I'm Emily Dupont. May I help you?"

Ashley quickly put out a hand. "Hi. I met Mr. Nicholson today and he told me I just had to come and see the shop. I'm Ashley."

"An art connoisseur?" Emily asked. She seemed to be an easy, relaxed person, happy where she was and eager to share art with others.

"Hardly." Ashley laughed. "I tend not to be too fond of modern art—or paintings called 'Black' that are just black. I pretty much fall in love with a piece or I don't. It might be a child's rendering or something hailed in the art world as the next great thing."

Emily laughed softly. "That's an art connoisseur to me. So how do you like the shop? And, by the way, I'm not here to pressure you. Just to help."

"Thank you."

Emily looked at Jake, who hadn't yet introduced himself.

"I'm Jake Mallory," he said. "I was here earlier today. I'm consulting with the police. We're going to solve the murder of Shelley Broussard."

Emily's smile faded. Tears sprang into her eyes. "Shelley," she whispered.

"I'm so sorry," Jake said.

Emily quickly wiped her face. "Sorry. We're trying to keep things going here. Sadly, eating and bill paying come out of working, and so... But poor Shelley. I still can't believe it."

"You were close friends," Ashley said.

"We lived together, we worked together. I loved her. She was a— sister." Emily paused to look around. The couple was still studying the painting of Royal Street or *Rue Royale*, as the painting had been titled. "I have no idea what she was doing, or where she was going, or... I just don't know."

"Why was she upset?" Jake asked her.

"Upset?"

Jake nodded. "Her murder was personal. She had a sign around her neck. It read *Traitor*. Who did she betray?"

Emily shook her head. "She didn't say anything to me. Or Samantha. Samantha is our other roommate. My other roommate now, I guess. We talked every night. Oh, we weren't wed to one another— we all went out with other friends and did our own thing. But we were together so often at night—as if we were back in high school and it was a slumber party."

"*I believe...but what is right is right, and what is wrong...is very wrong,*" Jake said.

"What's that?" Emily asked, frowning.

"Something Shelley wrote in her notebook," Jake said.

Ashley watched Emily as her face knit in consternation. She seemed to change color slightly—either baffled or disturbed.

"She was cheerful—she was supposed to meet Samantha and me the night she... The night she just disappeared."

"She didn't come home," Ashley said. "None of you were worried?"

"Well, she'd hinted that she'd met a man."

"I heard she'd fought with a man—maybe not fought, but had a negative response to him. Do you know who he was? A boyfriend?"

Ashley heard a door opening—not the front door, but a door in the back of the shop.

She looked up. The tall, dignified man she'd met earlier was coming in.

He might have been in the back—perhaps trying to listen to what was going on.

But now, he headed straight for them, beaming.

"Hello. And welcome. So, miss, you took me up on my invitation. The shop is wonderful, right?"

This time, Jake chose to identify himself. "Special Agent Jake Mallory, Mr. Nicholson. I met your wife earlier. And you happened to meet Ashley in the Square. We're about to head to a party, but saw the shop was open."

"We keep these doors open until eleven—we're on a street with clubs and restaurants and lots of people," Nicholson told him. "We do a great business when others might well be closed. No hardship on anyone, between our artists and my wife and myself. Anyway, what do you think?"

Ashley was surprised when Jake answered bluntly. "I'm surprised that you—that you had a young woman so close to you brutally murdered—and you're going about business as usual."

Emily gasped.

Nicholson's jaw locked for a moment.

"We have to keep living," he said finally. He pointed to the painting of the witch that had so captured Ashley. "We have to keep living, and we're trying to see that we can bury poor Shelley. You have your nerve, Special Agent."

"Sorry, I've just seen the crime photos," Jake said. "You don't have any video surveillance. Isn't that a bit...odd?"

"Careless, you mean," Nicholson said. "No. One of us is usually here."

"Can you tell me anything about this man who seemed to be after Shelley?" Jake asked.

"Oh." Nicholson inhaled and exhaled. "I'm going to say six-feet tall, or maybe six-one. Sandy blond/brown hair, short, but with kind of a piece that would go over his forehead now and then. Medium build. Twenties to, say..." He paused and looked at Emily.

"Twenties to thirties," Emily said. "He came in several times. He always asked for Shelley. She was nice to him, but I think he wanted more from her. I saw her get a little sharp with him one day. And he appeared to be upset."

"But you know nothing about him? Not even his name?" Jake asked.

"I'm afraid not," Nicholson said. "Emily?"

She shook her head. "No. Nothing. I'd ask her if she knew him, and she'd look a little upset and say he was just a pain—one of those customers who didn't really want anything except to bother the help."

"Thank you," Jake said. "Oh, by the way, was Shelley religious?"

Nicholson frowned. "Um, not that I know of."

"I think she was Catholic," Emily said. "I think I saw her go into the church by St. Louis."

"Our Lady of Guadalupe Chapel, on Rampart Street," Jake said.

"I guess," Emily murmured.

"Thank you," Jake said. "Thank you so much. Mr. Nicholson, I've been asked by the police to pick up Miss Broussard's notebook."

"Her notebook?" Nicholson asked.

"It's in her drawer upstairs."

"You were in my room?" Emily asked.

"With Mrs. Nicholson," Jake said.

"Oh, I see," Nicholson said. "Well, I'll go get it for you."

"I'll come with you, if you don't mind."

Nicholson was about to protest, Ashley was certain. "And while you two are up there, I'd like to talk to Emily about buying a painting. One of Shelley's paintings—I love it, and I'd like to help the cause as well." She spoke enthusiastically.

"Sir, let's get the notebook," Jake said. "Maybe there will be a clue to the young man harassing her."

Nicholson apparently decided protesting would make him appear to be defensive—or guilty of something. He shrugged. "All right."

When they were gone, Emily stared at Ashley. "You don't really want that painting," she accused.

"I do. I think it's haunting and beautiful. And tragic."

When Emily told her the price, Ashley realized she'd gotten a bit carried away with art that day. But it suddenly seemed incredibly important to her that she own the painting.

Because in that painting, Shelley had been saying something. Ashley was sure of it.

As she finished the transaction and Emily wrapped the painting, Jake and Nick Nicholson came back into the studio. Jake was thanking the man sincerely for his help and cooperation.

"Anything to help," Nicholson assured him.

When they were about to head out, Jake said, "Really, thank you. I haven't been able to reach Samantha Perkins, so I will be back. When is she working next?"

"Tomorrow, during the day," Emily answered.

"Thank you," Jake said.

"Oh, and I understand you've filled her space with that lovely and talented young woman we both met today," Ashley told Nicholson.

He nodded. "I try. I try to help all that I can."

"She's brilliant. She'll do well."

Emily was staring at Nicholson. She hadn't been told yet that their third had already been replaced.

Jake took Ashley by the arm. Thanking Emily and Nicholson again, they headed on out.

"You think something is going on there," Ashley said.

"Smells like a duck, looks like a duck..."

"But it would be impossible for his 'girls' to be the witches—Shelley was killed before the witches were even seen. And it could be crazy to associate the two murders. I mean, you said yourself Shelley was sweet. Tink was—well, he was pretty much a monster."

"Quacks like a duck," Jake said. "They bear watching. Now, what do you want to be for the party?"

"Uh, whatever. Anything."

"Except a witch." He muttered.

* * * *

Ashley had chosen to be a witch.

Not an ugly witch. Not a green witch with a huge hooked nose.

Instead, she'd found a costume that resembled the black gown worn by the girl in Shelley Broussard's painting.

"No." Jake didn't agree with her choice. At all.

"I can't possibly be mistaken for one of those creatures Tink saw. This is a good witch's outfit," Ashley said.

She stood on a little dais in the dressing room area, surrounded by mirrors. She was truly a beautiful witch. A jaunty black hat emphasized the gold in her hair. The raven-black color of the fabric enhanced the shimmering blue in her eyes.

There was no reason she shouldn't wear the costume, except...

She could have been the girl in the painting.

"What did you choose?" she asked.

He'd found a costume that was some kind of a movie rip-off. Black cape and black mask.

No one would know who he was.

"Ashley, I'm just in costume. While that…"

"I think it's important. Somehow."

The clerk approached, offering assistance. The costumes could be rented, but they were ridiculously cheap so Ashley said they'd purchase them.

Jake was still unhappy. Angry, even.

He wouldn't be having Ashley come to meet him here again, he determined.

They left the shop, heading to the parking lot he'd found to get the car. The streets were busy.

A crazed trio of murdering witches was alive and well, but Halloween and tourism must go on, he mused.

Maybe he was taking this one a little too closely. But rather than focus on that he slid behind the driver's seat to head to the refurbished warehouse in the CBD where the party was being held. He didn't speak as they drove.

"Jake, you're in danger all the time."

"And I've been through rigorous classes in self-defense."

"I've been with you through all of this for a long time."

He didn't answer her. Finding parking now was truly a project, so he concentrated on that instead. He had to drive around the area a few times and then slide into a parallel spot just as someone else was pulling out of it.

But they'd arrived. They could see others, dressed in all manner of costumes, ready to enjoy the party. He took Ashley's hand as they headed on in, stopping at the door for Jake to tell the bouncer they'd been invited by Sammy Riley.

Then they were in. And Jake started looking for witches—and trios.

Sammy found them almost instantly. He hugged Ashley and congratulated her, saying how glad he was they'd come. "Hey, some of the band guys are old friends of yours—yours too, Ashley. Remember when you were kids? Well, when we were all kids. Jake and his guitar. Both of you and your vocals."

"I was never going to be Jimmy Page," Jake said. Most people knew Page as one of the founders of the band Led Zeppelin, but Jake considered him to be the best guitar player in the world.

"He's a liar. He still plays all the time." Ashley laughed. "Three guitars in the living room alone."

"Maybe you could have been Jimmy Page," Sammy said. "But never mind. Jimmy Page is Jimmy Page."

"And I'm really satisfied and fulfilled with what I do," Jake said under his breath.

"Still, you could sit in," Sammy said. "And Ashley... Hey, man, maybe you could do that medley thing? That "Battle Hymn of the Republic with Dixie" riff you used to play. That would be really cool."

"Maybe. Think we'll hang for a while," Jake said.

"Sure. Have fun. See you in a bit. I'm on."

They made their way down to the floor before a large stage. The band introduced the "Ghouls at Halloween," and Sammy took part in a really cute little skit about ghouls who wanted to dress up as children to get candy for Halloween.

Jake half watched the stage.

And half watched the audience.

He realized someone was watching him as well.

It was a man dressed as a vampire—"Vampire Lestat," he realized, from the Anne Rice books. Such costumes were popular.

He was maybe just about six-feet. Average build.

Like half the males in the area.

But this guy looked as if he wanted to come and talk to Jake.

He almost moved over toward the man. But just then, Ashley tugged at his sleeve.

"Jake, there!"

He turned quickly.

A trio had come to stand near the stage, watching the players.

They weren't witches.

They were clowns.

Evil clowns. Well, he thought, it was a party filled with musicians, artists, and writers. The attendees were definitely honoring beloved authors such as Anne Rice and Steven King. The clowns might have come right out of a novel.

They were moving toward a man dressed as King Henry VIII. There was something about their movement that caught his attention.

"Stay here," Jake told Ashley.

He started their way, glad the gun in his holster was his own bureau-issued Glock and not the costume piece that had come with the outfit. His black cape covered the truth of it.

It wasn't easy getting through the crowd.

Even as he neared them, the clowns had moved. One of them had seen him. And known. Known that he was coming for them.

The clowns turned and started heading out.

They'd be heading straight toward Ashley.

He changed his own pace. And as the clowns seemed to converge on Ashley, he shouted out. "FBI! Get down!"

His words were met with applause and laughter. It was, after all, a costume party.

The clowns were almost upon Ashley. They stopped. And they stared.

Something about her—or the costume she was wearing—had given them pause.

They broke apart—twenty feet from Ashley.

And began to run.

Jake went after them. Logic said he had to go after the closest, but even the closest was blocked by a throng of people.

Ashley was safe—from the clowns at least.

Jake burst out onto the street. "Where'd the clowns go?" he demanded of the bouncer.

"The clowns? Buddy, this place is full of clowns."

He saw one down the street and ran. This clown stopped, terrified, as Jake reached him and caught him by the arm.

"Hey, hey, what's wrong?"

The clown was a young man—high school age. He was purely terrified, and seeing his face now and the makeup on it, Jake knew he hadn't been one of the masked clowns that had drawn his attention inside.

Beaten, he determined to find his way back to Ashley as quickly as possible.

He needed to do three things. Get to Ashley. Find out just who the hell was wearing the Henry VIII costume. And figure out why in hell the clowns would have been after him.

Chapter 6

Clowns, not witches.

But a trio.

And Ashley had seen clearly they were heading for the man dressed elegantly as Henry VIII.

They had been coming her way. And they stopped—as if stunned—when they'd seen her. Why? Because she'd resembled the woman in the painting?

It might be a stretch of the imagination, but with Jake out on the street—hopefully catching a clown—she moved through the still-laughing crowd toward the stage, listening.

"That was great," someone said. "An FBI guy in a cape chasing clowns."

"Isn't that life?" someone else replied.

"This party gets better every year. You just never know what you'll see. Performances all around," another woman said.

Ashley was by them. King Henry VIII was up near the stage, clapping. The performance had just ended and the band was picking back up where it had left off—now playing a Journey song.

Henry VIII turned from the stage and the thudding music to Ashley. She couldn't tell much about him—he was wearing a wig, cap, and fake facial hair—but he seemed to quickly size her up.

"Hello," he said. "I'm Richard Showalter. Nice to meet you. And you are...?"

"Ashley," she said. He didn't really want her last name. He was thinking about the direction in which the night might take them.

She hesitated, not sure how to ask a man why three evil clowns might want to kill him.

"Did you—see the clowns?" she asked.

"Yeah. Cool costumes."

"They seemed focused on you."

"Maybe they're fans."

"Oh? What do you do?" Ashley asked him.

"Well, I blog. Mainly. I have a few books out, too. Nonfiction. The state of man and all that. You're sure you've never heard of me? I'm on local TV often enough."

"I'm sorry. The state of man. What exactly do you see the state of man being?"

"Well, it's rather sad, to be honest. I was just on TV—local network affiliate—talking against some of the laws being bandied about. Florida—and that 'stand your ground' thing. People are taking the law into their own hands. And, because of it, other people are being murdered. It's not a self-defense thing. Okay, so yes, we get crime waves. But then you get idiots out there who want to shoot up the crooks. And end up shooting others. Or baiting crooks to come on over and get shot. I did a great piece on supporting our local police, bolstering them up instead of tearing them down."

She stared at him, wondering where to go from there. Was someone in the city wanting to murder crooks—and then, maybe, murder Richard Showalter for not wanting crooks to be murdered in the street?

But that brought them back to Shelley Broussard. She was no crook.

She didn't have to say anything more. Jake was back, panting a little. Obviously concerned as he caught up to her.

"This is Richard Showalter. He writes a blog," Ashley told him and studied his reaction. He shook his head slightly.

He hadn't caught up with any clowns.

"And I have several books out," Showalter said, shouting to be heard over the music. He was being polite, not necessarily interested in the conversation any more—now that another man was involved. He knew he wasn't going to be taking Ashley home with him.

"About?" Jake asked.

At least Showalter's ego was such that he had to stay and tell Jake what he did.

Jake didn't hesitate.

"I think those clowns were about to kill you," he said flatly.

"Hey, I'm not your size but I'm not a shrinking violet either. I could have held my own—until security reached me, at least. Until the law stepped in."

"No," Jake said. "They didn't mean to beat you up. They wanted to slit your throat."

"Ah, come on, it's Halloween," Showalter said, clearly not taking the threat seriously. "But really, enough is enough. You two are obviously together. If you don't mind, I'd kind of like to meet a new friend tonight."

Jake pulled out his credentials.

"Where'd you buy that? Looks real," Showalter said.

"It is real," Jake snapped, his patience evidently on edge. "You heard about the witches who killed the man the other day."

"Of course."

"Well, I believe that was them."

"Those were clowns."

"Oh, good God!" Jake exploded. "They were dressed up as witches. Now they're dressed up as clowns. And they seem to have a vendetta against you. They were heading straight for you."

"Witches, clowns, whatever. I'm not a criminal," Showalter said indignantly. His confidence, however, seemed to be fraying. "The guy who was killed... He was a criminal. Sure, that's my platform—people just can't take the law into their own hands. It's against everything we stand for as Americans. And it causes more and more damage. Oh, my God." He stopped, his face draining of color as the situation became clear to him. "Do you really think that they were the killers and... You think they wanted to kill me? Right here? Now? In this crowd?"

"It's damned possible," Jake said.

The demeanor of the man had changed completely. "So—so what do I do now? I don't own a gun. I'm not a violent man. I can't even leave here. They could be waiting for me. And I won't even know them. I don't know if they'll be witches or clowns or just people walking down the street. I don't even know if they were men or women."

Good call, Ashley thought. It was true. From what she understood, the witches' makeup had concealed any concept of a real face, and the clowns had been wearing masks. They could have been male or female or a mix.

"You have to protect me. You have to." Richard Showalter was working himself into a panic.

But it was true. He was now their responsibility. Ashley looked over at Jake.

They both knew it was true.

"Where do you live?" Jake asked.

"Garden District."

"Okay. You have a car here?"

"Took an Uber. I knew I'd drink."

"All right. We'll get you there, and then I'll have the cops watching your place. Please tell me you don't put your real address out anywhere," Jake said.

"No, I use a P.O. box," Showalter said.

"Thank God for small favors," Jake muttered.

They all turned to leave. The music stopped and Ashley turned again, looking back at the stage. Sammy Riley was up there now, and he called out to her loudly. "Hey, Ashley—where are you guys going? Thought you were going to come on up and do a number."

"Next time, Sammy," Ashley called.

"That's next year," Sammy said.

"Next year then," Ashley said cheerfully and waved.

She wished he hadn't called out to her, drawing attention to her and Jake and Richard Showalter.

"Hey," Showalter said, balking.

"What?" Jake asked.

"Are you guys just fooling with me? You're musicians? Is this all a crock—is that I.D. of yours a costume piece?"

"I'm an agent who loves his guitar. The badge is real."

"It's real," Ashley swore. "I don't know what to say to convince you. We need to see you're—safe."

Showalter sighed. "So help me, if this isn't the truth... If you hurt me, kill me, I'll... I'll haunt the hell out of you."

Ashley smiled. "Join the party," she murmured.

"Let's go," Jake said firmly.

"All right, all right." Showalter moved.

And Ashley still hesitated, just a second.

They had been watching people. They'd come to watch people.

But she was afraid that people might have been watching them too. It was just a feeling, but...

She shook her head and stopped that line of thought, hurrying out behind the men.

"I'm not a violent man. I don't even carry a gun," Showalter muttered as they went.

"Not to worry. I do," Jake assured him.

The streets were busy. Jake urged Ashley and Showalter ahead of him until they reached the car. Once in, Jake got Showalter's address and they drove the distance.

Showalter's street in the Garden District was quiet at night. Stately old residences—most of them fenced, and most with alarm systems—sat quietly in the night like the Old Guard.

"There's an alarm system?" Jake asked.

"Of course," Showalter said.

"Excellent."

"You have a dog?" Ashley asked.

"Sorry, I have a cat. A guard cat—honestly. I have a huge old mutt cat I think has some wild cat mixed in. He'll go after you."

Showalter opened the gate with his key and they followed him up to a handsome Georgian residence. He hesitated just a second, then opened the front door and stepped inside, hitting numbers on the alarm pad just inside the door.

"I'm confused. Are you staying? I mean, you're not leaving me, right? Killer clowns, or witches. Or... Damn."

"Jake will call the NOPD," Ashley assured Showalter. "They'll see that someone comes to watch out for you."

"I don't want just anyone in my house. Wait a minute. A good cop—a really good cop. Sure—he can be in my house. I mean, you're not just going to get a cop to drive by every hour, or anything like that, right?"

Jake ignored him and stepped away to organize things on the phone.

Ashley watched him and tried to chat with Showalter too, aware he was actually making two calls.

"I love this place," she said. And she did. The architectural style was one of her favorites.

"Me too. It's real vintage New Orleans. My grandparents owned it. I used to come for summers, but I grew up in Chicago. Dad's job."

"Chicago is a great city, world class jazz and blues and museums and more," Ashley said.

"Yes, that's true. But I always loved this place. And I'm an only grandchild so it was mine if I wanted it. I work from home and I can handle the upkeep. My folks aren't retired yet. They come when they can. As you can see, it's plenty big."

"You have no live-in help?"

He shook his head. "No. I have two housekeepers, but they come every couple of days. It's just me. Not that big a mess." He seemed to want answers then. "A guitar-playing G-man, huh? And you?"

"Jake and I have known each other since we were kids. We were in a band together at one time."

"And now?"

"We live in Virginia."

"But you're locals."

"Yes." She shrugged and decided to say at last, "My name is Ashley Donegal."

"Wow. Wow. Nice! I mean this house, I love it, but Donegal Plantation, that's cool. Really cool." He frowned. "They have G-men working on plantations now?"

"Trust me—NOLA has an office. With great agents. But Jake is part of a special unit. They're in Virginia."

"I see. I think."

Jake came back to them, finished with his calls. "We'll be splitting things up for the next twenty-four hours. NOPD and FBI," he explained. "Officer Jacobs will be here soon."

"How do we know we can trust him?" Showalter asked.

Jake frowned. "I thought you were all for the police."

"I am."

"So?"

"Can we trust him?" Showalter asked anxiously.

"I think so. He's the nephew of the lead detective on the case—Detective Parks. Parks is great and intuitive—I'm glad to be helping him out. If he's sending his nephew, he trusts his nephew."

"And then?"

"Tomorrow, you'll have a Krewe escort until...well, until we get where we need to be and you're safe."

"Krewe? Hey, it's not Mardi Gras. I don't need—"

"Krewe of Hunters. It's a moniker for my special unit. You'll be in good hands," Jake promised him.

Showalter walked to the bar cart and offered them a drink. They refused.

"Fine. I'll drink alone. No problem."

He sat down, then nearly leapt up three feet when he heard the buzzer from his gate.

"That's Jacobs," Ashley said softly.

"Oh, okay. The key is there." He pointed to the coffee table.

Ashley started to get it but Jake was ahead of her, sweeping it up and going back out to open the gate.

"I'm Larry Jacobs," the young man in uniform was saying as Jake led him into the room. "Detective Parks sent me. Guard duty."

He was young, lithe, and looked to be sharp as a tack. His hair was reddish and his eyes were a deep, intense brown. He looked around briefly and then asked, "Alarm system?"

"Yes," Jake said, then he hesitated. "I don't think anyone will come for him here—alarms cause a ruckus, though even the most sophisticated can be thwarted. This is precautionary. Just in case."

"Understood. Nice to meet you," Jacobs said to Ashley.

"A pleasure. And thank you," Ashley said.

He nodded and held a hand out to Richard Showalter, who immediately offered him a drink.

"Not while I'm looking after you, sir," Jacobs said.

Showalter seemed to appraise him, then nodded to Jake. "I like this kid."

"Good. He'll be with you until tomorrow, mid-morning. And don't worry, someone else will be with you then," Jake assured him.

"Until you all get tired of watching out for me, right?" Showalter took a swig of his drink.

"We don't get tired of watching out for people," Jake said.

Richard Showalter lifted his drink in a mock toast to Ashley. "And to think, for a moment I thought I was going to have a magical night."

"It was a magical night," Jake said curtly. "You're alive."

Showalter's hand shook as he hastily put his drink down, slopping whiskey. "Yes, you're right. Thank you both. I think." He grimaced. "Maybe they were just clowns."

"Good night," Ashley told him softly.

"Goodnight, y'all," Larry Jacobs called, and they bid him good night as well.

When they left, Ashley asked Jake, "You really do think the clowns were the witches, right?"

"Yeah, I do," he told her. "They ran like hell when they saw me—

instinct, I guess. I haven't figured it out yet, but…"

"Vigilantes," Ashley said. Jake seemed distant and—she thought—still upset with her. "But where does Shelley fit in? Or does she?"

Jake didn't answer. "Tomorrow. I'll get back on it tomorrow."

He had said "*I'll.*"

She wasn't being invited into the city tomorrow.

She understood his worry. The clowns had stopped when they saw her. And the outfit she had chosen did resemble the one worn by the woman in the painting by Shelley she had purchased. The painting now in the backseat of the car.

When they reached Donegal, she was exhausted. "I'm going on up," she said softly.

He stood in the foyer—between the two winding staircases where she had planned for them to marry—lost in thought.

"Jake?"

"I'll be up in a bit," he said.

But he wasn't.

She showered and lay awake. He didn't come.

But the dream did come. Again.

She was back on Bourbon Street, once more headed from Canal toward Esplanade. Hawkers were about, people laughing and talking. Music blared.

She knew now she was searching for the young woman. And suddenly there she was, the pretty blonde with the huge brown eyes.

"Please," the girl whispered again.

"Are you Shelley?" Ashley asked.

The question startled her. "I… Shelley. Yes, I'm Shelley. And I'm so frightened and so lost. Please…"

"Oh, Shelley, I'm so sorry."

"I'm dead. I know I'm dead. I don't… I don't know…"

"Who did this to you?"

"I'm… I'm lost. I felt it. I was so afraid. I painted it, in the picture. I could feel it, and it was wrong and there was something… I wanted to find out. Oh…" She was looking down the street. Ashley turned.

The mist, the black mist like a massive wave of ravens' wings, was coming again.

And soon, the girl would disappear.

"Wait!" Ashley cried.

But the apparition was gone. And the ebony darkness seemed to be coming closer and closer.

She woke with a start. Jake must have come to bed at last because he woke instantly at her gasp.

"Ashley?"

"I'm sorry. I didn't mean to disturb you."

"A dream? A nightmare?"

He was already worried about the costume she had chosen. About the way the clowns had stopped and looked at her.

"No, I just rolled wrong and woke myself up," she lied.

He pulled her into his arms. "I love you so much," he whispered.

"I love you."

He held her. In time, they made love.

She didn't sleep again.

When his phone rang the next morning, Ashley knew that it was going to be a very long day.

Chapter 7

It had taken some time, but sitting in Parks' office at the station, Jake finally got through to Mrs. Alice Hunt—Shelley Broussard's mother.

The woman answered the phone impatiently. She didn't sound like someone who had just lost a beloved family member.

"Mrs. Hunt, this is Special Agent Mallory with the FBI."

"FBI? I thought the police were investigating. She was murdered in New Orleans. Who are you? Is this a prank?"

He stared at the phone. "This is no prank. Are you really Miss Broussard's mother?"

There was a surprising silence on the other end.

"No."

"No?"

"Shelley was the child of my ex-husband's no-good sister. We were getting married, so... Well, you know. We adopted her legally. But was I really her mother? No."

Did that explain it? Could anything explain someone being so cold about the murder of a child they had raised?

"All right." He changed his approach. "Did Shelley Broussard grow up with you?"

"Yes. Until she was seventeen and she ran away. Then my no-good husband ran away. I remarried soon after. I have three children under the age of five, Special Agent whomever. If that's who you really are. I can't just drop everything for a girl who basically kicked up her heels eight years ago and left."

"Why did she leave?"

"Her father was crazy."

Her father—not you? Jake found himself feeling very sorry for the three children under five.

"All right. Are you coming to New Orleans?"

"I've spoken to a woman who will have her interred in a family tomb in New Orleans. There's no reason for me to come. I mean, she's dead already. Not like I can help."

"Well, maybe you can help. Without coming to New Orleans. Can you give me the names of any of Shelley's friends when you still saw her?"

The woman was quiet. For a moment, Jake thought that she was going to refuse to help.

Then she mumbled, "A bunch of wackos."

"Why do you say that?" Jake asked.

"Who the hell else pays for a stranger's funeral and interment?" the woman asked.

Jake heard a dog barking and a child crying—then another child jabbering.

"I've got to go," Mrs. Hunt said.

"I understand. But please, just one name." He hated to beg, but it would be worth it if she could provide a lead.

"Katey," she sighed. "Katey DuLac. They were friends for years. Pen pals and such. She lived in New Orleans but visited her grandparents here in Houston every summer. And when she did, the girls were inseparable." She paused. "That's all I know. Please don't call again."

And she hung up.

Jake shook his head and stared at the phone. He still couldn't grasp the uncaring attitude, but focused on the small bit of information she'd provided.

He tried directory assistance first, looking for a Katey or Katherine DuLac. No luck. Then he called Angela Hawkins—Jackson Crow's right hand, second in command, and master of research. Not to mention his wife. She, like Jake, had been part of the original Krewe team.

On the first case.

Where it all began. Right here in New Orleans.

"Jackson is on his way," Angela assured him.

"I know. I need your help."

"Okay."

"Katey or Katherine DuLac. She was from Orleans Parish. She'd be about twenty-five now."

"I'm on it."

He hung up and concentrated on the crime board he'd prepared with Detective Parks. Pictures of the dead man and the dead woman in life—and then in death. When their bodies had been discovered, and once again, at the morgue.

One a crook. One a well-liked artist—with a wretched past, or so it seemed. There was information about Tink, about his arrest record. And there was information about Shelley's work and "Picture This."

But he wanted more information on Marty and Nick Nicholson.

An idea occurred to him and he picked up his phone. But even as he did so, he saw that Angela was calling back.

"She's still in New Orleans," Angela reported. "Her name is now Katherine Willoughby. She's in the Bywater area." She gave him the exact address and a phone number.

Jake thanked her. "I'm going to go out and see her. Will you check something else for me?"

"Go," Angela said.

He asked her for information on Marty and Nick Nicholson—and on murders of known criminals. "In New Orleans and surrounding areas—and in Houston, Texas."

"You think that these people are killing crooks?" Angela asked.

"Maybe. I'm going to go through what they have at the station here, but you seem to have a magic touch."

"You know how to flatter," Angela told him. "By the way, how are the wedding plans going?"

"Um, great."

"We all can't wait, you know. Jackson has arranged for the newest recruits to hold down the fort, so he and I..."

"Yes?"

She laughed. "Hopefully, it will be a beautiful wedding for you and Ashley. And then, Jackson and I intend on a little honeymoon of our own."

"Sounds great," Jake assured her.

When he hung up, his thoughts were conflicted. He was determined to see if his theory was correct. He wanted to find out what had been going on since the Nicholson duo had come to town and started recruiting struggling artists.

And he was worried too. Haunted by the way Ashley had looked in the costume.

Concerned about the way the clowns had stopped and stared at her.

He found himself praying that there would be a wedding. He was so worried that he wanted to drop everything and run back to her.

She'd be furious, of course. He picked up the phone instead. He was relieved when she answered right away.

"Hey, how's it going there?"

"Great," she assured him. "I went for a ride this morning. I really miss having horses."

"Maybe we can figure something out. There are stables not that far from us. Not the same as having them right outside your door, but..."

"We'll see. I know that Varina is happy here."

"She'd be happy anywhere. With you. Like me."

"Ah, that's sweet. Anyway, I'm watching some of the quickie rehearsals for tonight—and then, later, I'll be on porch duty with Beth. I might even check out the real stuff going on. I looked us up on some social media sites—we're really cool. Five stars all over."

"Great," he told her, relieved. She sounded fine.

"How are you doing?" she asked him. "Any luck? Anywhere?"

"I'm going to try to find an old friend of Shelley Broussard. See what she has to say."

"Good. I got a strange vibe from that man—Nick Nicholson. He comes across so polished. Kind, dignified. Dedicated to the arts and to young, struggling artists. The type of people who are in abundance in New Orleans. But there's just something about him."

"I agree. Jackson is coming in. Our local office has a team of men out on the streets with the cops. Hopefully there will be enough men—and women—to take down that trio when they show up next. In whatever costume they choose to wear."

"I hope so. And don't worry. I'm working here. You do your work—catch these horrible people. I'm fine and I won't be alone," she assured him. "I am busy, busy, busy, too."

He smiled at her ability to soothe him and lighten the mood at the same time. She was the best, always. And as dedicated to the Krewe as he was. Determined to let him use his talents. First to save lives. And then to find justice for those that had been lost.

"Love you," he said.

"You, too."

He hung up. He was heading out to see Katey. Katherine DuLac Willoughby. And he hoped that she was the key.

For all their sakes.

* * * *

Ashley wasn't busy. She'd been preparing an attraction with Cliff, but now she was in her room.

Studying the painting.

The painting created by Shelley Broussard.

Ashley realized, following news reports *and* her dream, that Shelley had painted a big-eyed version of herself in the scene. And equally, she knew why Jake had been so upset last night. She and Shelley had been built alike. True, her eyes were blue while Shelley's had been a deep brown, but they both had long blonde hair, worn almost the same way. In the costume…

She might have looked like a ghost to the killers.

The very ghost now haunting her dreams.

Staring at the picture was getting her nowhere. She was convinced that she was right, and she knew that the ghost was trying to reach her, but only seemed to touch her dreams.

"Why me, Shelley?" she whispered to the picture. "And do you know what? I'm pretty good at this ghost thing. I don't immediately think I'm crazy—or start to pass out the second I see a ghost. You need to speak to me. You need to tell me what happened to you."

The picture was silent.

Over time, Ashley had learned that the dead were very much like the living. Some were outgoing. Some were confused. Some were shy. Some could manifest easily, and some could not.

She continued to stare pensively at the painting. Maybe Shelley Broussard hadn't learned how to manifest herself into something seeable—hearable. She was a "new" ghost, and perhaps no one out there had helped her yet, shown her the ropes… So she wasn't good at being seen or heard yet.

Sometimes it was possible to get close to the dead by touching their bodies.

Ashley walked out onto the balcony, thoughtful as she looked over her property. She had to get into the morgue. That sounded ghoulish, but they were running out of options.

And Shelley needed to be heard.

Just as the thought came to her, she saw one of the giant spiders creeping up the column and some of the ghosts clinging to the railing of the wraparound porch. Everyone preparing for the festivities.

In truth, she wasn't a ghoul, but she did need to get into the morgue. If she just went back into the city, Jake would get her in.

He wouldn't like it, having been unnerved by the clowns staring at her last night, but he'd do it.

She'd promised that she'd stay here tonight. But sometimes promises needed to be broken when help was needed. And for some reason, she knew she had to help Shelley.

As she weighed her options, a car swung onto the property and pulled into the area to the far right of the house where a sign read *Cast Parking*. It carried several of their scare actors for the coming night. Evidently, their "witches" knew one another.

Three women and one man emerged from the car. She recognized Lavinia Carole, Valerie Deering, and Rhonda Blackstone from the staff meeting. The man was Jonathan Starling—looking young and very *normal*—by day.

Another car drove into the lot.

Ashley realized that it was afternoon, and it was getting close to time for the cast and crew to get ready for the night. If she was going into the city of New Orleans, she was going to have to hurry.

* * * *

Katherine Willoughby—nee DuLac—was at the door when he arrived, evidently as anxious to talk with him as he had been to speak with her.

"Jake Mallory. Nice to meet you—in the flesh," she told him.

She was a woman with a quick and beautiful smile, of medium height, a little on the plump side, with a charming, cherub's face. "I followed your exploits when you were in high school. Pretty impressive. I know we've never met, but I had a crush on you through the local section of the papers. You were so—sporty."

He grinned, shaking her hand. She wasn't just plump, he realized. She was pregnant.

"Well, thank you. And thank you for this. For seeing me."

Katey no longer smiled. "Come in. I have coffee on."

They sat in her kitchen—a place freshly painted in shades of yellow and blue, homey and comfortable.

"I was stunned when I heard about what had happened to Shelley. She was... Shelley was so incredible. She loved everyone, helped everyone... And she might have made it big. She was really an amazing artist. She used to do paintings at Mardi Gras time, people in masks and costumes. From the time we were little kids, she loved painting."

"Did you two keep up with one another?"

Katey stood and walked over to the refrigerator. She moved a magnet and some coupons there and came back to the table with a sketch. It was of a toddler, smiling. A little boy with golden curls that resembled Katey—a small Katey.

"She sent me that a little while ago. She was going to come and stay here with me a bit after the baby was born."

"So you were close?"

"Not really. I seldom saw her lately. She was so busy, working all the time. But she was happy. The other girls had promised to cover her shifts at the studio so that she could stay a week with me. My mom can come—she's living in Houston now—but if she waits that one week, she'll be cleared from her job to stay a whole month."

"I see." And he did. They hadn't seen much of each other lately, but they had still been good friends. And Katey had loved Shelley Broussard.

"You never called the police?" he asked her.

She hesitated. "My husband said that I needed to stay out of it. And as far away from anything to do with Shelley as I could. For the baby."

"But you're seeing me now," Jake said gently.

She inhaled. "You called me. I had to see you. And I did love Shelley."

"Why was your husband afraid? Do you—know something?" He decided to push her a bit. "She was found with a sign around her neck. A sign that read *Traitor.*"

Katey hesitated. "If I really knew anything, I would have called."

"But something is bothering you. Was there trouble where she was working? At the art gallery?"

Katey arched her brows. "No, she loved the gallery. They were giving her a real opportunity. Do you know how many artists flock to New Orleans and vie for space and sales around Jackson Square?

Making a name as an artist isn't easy—especially here. The competition is fierce. It's a great community for artists, but making a living isn't easy. No, she loved the gallery."

"Was there a man who might have done this?"

"There was someone she was seeing. And then not seeing. She was disturbed because he kept coming into the studio."

"Did you ever meet him? Do you have a name for me?"

"Yes, I do." She stilled and her tone dropped. "Jonathan. Jonathan Starling."

Chapter 8

Ashley didn't tell anyone but Beth that she was leaving. The players were all assembling, costuming and preparing for the evening, and she would be back soon.

When she returned, she'd change into costume. Something that she had worn during the re-enactment days, or maybe... Maybe she'd wear the outfit that had so upset the clowns. She couldn't imagine that her killing trio would be headed this far into the country, away from the prime pickings of the city. But if they did, the plantation had security working and a county police officer on duty every night.

She'd worry about that later. Right now she had to get into NOLA.

She called an Uber again. It wasn't until she was nearly in the city that she called Jake.

He answered, sounding surprised to hear from her.

"What's up?" she asked, trying to sound casual.

"I'm trying to pin down the location of a man. The boyfriend. And I'm waiting for Jackson."

"Jackson is on his way?"

"Yep. With Jude McCoy."

"Nice." Jude McCoy was a more recent addition to the Krewe, but he hailed from New Orleans and was great. He had first worked with Jackson on a serial killer case when the killer found refuge on a cruise ship out of New Orleans. He was intuitive—fast as an arrow—and a great friend and agent.

"You know how we like to do things. One will watch over Richard Showalter and one will work with me."

"What about the cops?"

"They're short officers in the city right now and they also have to deal with Halloween. Jackson calls the shots and this is how he's called it. Jude is friends with a lot of the local agents who will be prowling the city, so it's a good call. But how are you? How's it going at the property?"

She looked ahead. The Uber driver was ever-so-slightly dancing to a number by Queen that was playing on his radio.

"I'm on my way in," Ashley told him.

"What?" Snapping anger and disbelief were clear in his voice.

"I need to see Shelley Broussard's corpse," Ashley said.

"No, you don't," Jake responded instantly.

"Listen to me. She's the ghost I'm seeing in my dreams, Jake. This is important."

"What makes you think it's her?"

"My eyesight. I look like her—especially when I'm dressed up in that costume that resembles the one worn in the painting she did. Jake, come on. She may really know something. She could help us."

"Don't come in, Ashley."

"I'm almost there."

He was silent for so long, Ashley thought he'd hung up on her. Then she heard a long sigh.

"Have the driver take you straight to the morgue," he said, obviously still irritated. But he would meet her. And she knew that meant he believed her.

She agreed and they ended the call.

She hadn't told the driver that she was headed to the morgue—she'd just given him the address.

But apparently he'd found the connection.

"You're going to the morgue?" he asked, his eyes catching hers in the mirror.

"Yes," she said.

"I've never taken anyone to the morgue before."

"I guess that's good."

She didn't tell him more. He was probably wondering if she'd been called in to identify a body, but she couldn't very well tell him the truth.

So she sat in silence for the next twenty minutes of the ride.

They arrived and he let her out on the curb. She studied the building and felt a moment of sadness at its function. New Orleans had excellent pathologists and medical examiners by necessity. The city—and the entire parish—had been through a lot.

She headed up the path. Before she reached the front door, Jake stepped out. And he wasn't alone. Jackson Crow walked at his side.

Their tall, seemingly impregnable leader had been an agent before the birth of the Krewe. He was imposing in his stature and appearance, with features that spoke to his Native American and Northern European heritage. He could be stoic—his position often demanded it—but it was his gentle streak that Ashley admired.

He must have just arrived.

She was glad. Jackson would make this easier.

Jake was visibly angry. He didn't speak. Jackson greeted her with a kiss on the cheek and a worried smile. "You know what you're doing, right, Ashley? I hate to remind you, but you're a civilian."

"You use other civilians when the need calls for it," she reminded him.

Jake was standing tall and straight by Jackson's side. They were both rather towering.

At least Jackson seemed to be on her side.

"Let's go in," he said.

They met up with Detective Parks, who had apparently made arrangements, and they were immediately ushered down a long hall and into one of the holding chambers. The autopsy had been completed, but Shelley Broussard had been brought out on a rolling gurney for them to see. She waited in the center of one of the examination rooms.

The medical examiner seemed curious, but she kept that curiosity to herself. She introduced herself as Dr. Sienna Hardgrave.

Shelley lay with a stark white sheet drawn up to her breasts. The gash in her throat was obvious. There was a sweetness and innocence about her face.

Even in death.

Ashley swallowed hard.

"Dr. Hardgrave has explained," Jake said, "that Shelley was most likely taken from behind. Like this—" Jackson moved forward, allowing Jake to demonstrate how the killer had come up from behind, taking her by surprise, holding her by her shoulder with his left hand, and drawing the knife hard across the throat with the right.

"She never saw her killer," Jackson said.

"Miss Donegal." Detective Parks focused on her. "Do you know something?"

She shook her head. "I just—by coincidence—met the man who owns the gallery where she was living and working. And I bought one of her paintings. I'm sorry to have disturbed everyone coming here, but…" She paused, shaking her head. "I can't help but feel that I'm getting to know her and that there are clues in her life or in the painting. The killer had to have been someone close to her. Someone she trusted, and someone who would call her a traitor." She stepped forward, trying not to let the M.E. or the detective see that she wanted to touch Shelley's body.

And see if she could reach the ghost haunting her dreams.

The dead were cold. So cold. And yet, even as she stood there touching the frigid flesh of the deceased, she imagined that she saw the young woman open her eyes, look at her, and whisper softly, "Please help me."

The intensity of the plea was heart wrenching.

Ashley jolted and stepped back.

Jake didn't miss the response. He moved forward, blocking Ashley while thanking the medical examiner, and guided her toward the door.

On the street, he spoke. Not angrily, but in anguish. "Ashley…"

He was visibly shaken on her behalf, reminding her that even when angry, he'd never be anything but…Jake.

"Jude is at our office here in town," Jackson said. "Let's go talk. She needs to know exactly what we know."

Ashley looked at Jake and frowned, confused. He'd been upset on the phone that she was coming in.

What had happened since they'd talked?

"You shouldn't be at home, either. Not without…one of us. Not until we've had a chance to talk," Jackson said quietly.

"Let's head to your office," Detective Parks said. As head of the investigation, he was definitely joining the party.

Parks had his own car and Jackson rode with him, leaving Ashley alone with Jake in their rental car.

After clicking in her seatbelt, Ashley turned to him, determined to get some answers. "Jake, what's going on?"

He looked at her unhappily.

"Since you spoke with me," she persisted.

"Two things, Ashley. Angela has been doing research back at Krewe headquarters."

"And?"

He inhaled. "She found a number of deaths from here to Biloxi and over in Baton Rouge that had been chalked up to drugs or gang violence. Bad guys—really bad guys—were killed. Murdered. She found seven in all, over the last year and a half."

"So you think whoever killed that man Tink and most probably Shelley Broussard—and went after Richard Showalter—murdered those people as well?"

"Quite possibly. They see themselves as vigilantes. Shelley might have known about them—and not wanted to be involved."

"The art studio," Ashley said.

"Yes. But I also found out the name of the man she kept seeing at the gallery. The one who'd given her a hard time."

"You did?"

"She told an old friend about him. An old friend that she hadn't seen much of since she started at the gallery."

"And his name is—?"

"His name is Jonathan Starling. According to Angela, he's one of your employees at Donegal for the Halloween season—a scare actor. So, you see, on the one hand, I don't want you getting involved here in the city. You might have put a target on yourself. But I don't exactly want you out there, either—not until we find out just what went on with this man. With Jonathan Starling."

Chapter 9

Jake watched Ashley as she stared at the crime board. It held pictures, facts, figures, theories, and more.

In many ways, it caused a serious conflict of feeling—some very bad people had been murdered. So it had been easy for various agencies to believe they'd been killed because of gang wars or drug deals gone wrong. But...

Each one had had their throat slit.

Ashley was shaking her head. "I can't believe this. I mean, it's all too confusing. What? The art studio people—Nick Nicholson and Marty—bring in these girls and then try to make a trio of killers out of them? Okay, they killed Tink around Halloween so they could be witches. They went after Richard Showalter as clowns—because it was Halloween? But how did they sneak up on hardened criminals? And if they were after criminals, why kill poor Shelley? And what does Jonathan Starling have to do with any of this?"

"I don't know," Jake told her.

"And what about Richard Showalter? Is he being protected? Do we even know that the clowns were really after him?"

"No," Jake told her. "But don't worry. We're keeping him protected."

"NOPD and the cops are sharing the responsibility of watching out for him," Detective Parks added.

Jackson reached over and touched Ashley's hand. "I know this is all a mess. For now, we have Jude hanging out with Showalter. The three of us want to go back to the plantation with you. They're setting up for tonight, right? So this man who was bothering Shelley—this Jonathan Starling—will be there?"

"Oh, yes, along with goblins—and witches. We have our own witches. Three of them," Ashley said dryly.

"Three witches?" Jake said.

"Yes. The old kitchen is a gingerbread house—and there are three witches in it. They have a clever setup. One of the witches ends up shoved into an oven, which is really just a little back room that allows her to exit to the grounds. When one group is finished, she pops back in so that it can all be repeated with the next one. We have that, and the smokehouse, and the haunted hayride." She hesitated. "The haunted smokehouse—where Jonathan is working—is really something. Body pieces, heads on shelves… It's just great." She ended with a whisper.

It was Halloween.

Halloween was great in New Orleans.

Great at Donegal Plantation.

Chills, thrills, and fantasy.

But now it would all be tainted.

With very real murders.

"Thursday night," Jackson murmured. "And Halloween on Tuesday."

"You think they're gearing up for something big?" Jake asked him.

Jackson shrugged. "They've been at this awhile—if our theories are correct. And they didn't make any mistakes. Until they killed Shelley. And left a witness."

"You okay?" Jake asked Ashley.

She nodded.

"Did you…"

"Feel anything from touching her?" she whispered, glancing at Detective Parks.

He just looked back at her, curious.

She shook her head. "But…at the morgue… The way you showed how she was taken. I think that was right. I think that she was worried about something happening, but that she didn't think she was in danger herself."

"*I believe…but what is right is right, and what is wrong…is very wrong,*" Jake murmured and then spoke to the room. "I'd like to give this a go. Ashley, Jackson, and I will head back and pretend that we're paying attention to what's happening at Donegal because it's Ashley's home. We'll speak casually with this man—Jonathan Starling. And I'd like to meet the rest of the scare actors out there, too. Especially the witches. Then, after we've had a chance to be casual, we might be able to cause some interesting reactions to any questions regarding Shelley Broussard."

It was agreed. Jake, Jackson, and Ashley headed out. She was pensive all the while.

"What?" Jake asked her.

"I don't understand." She glanced at Jackson, and he knew that she would speak more freely now.

While there was plenty of speculation about the Krewe, none of its members ever admitted to talking to the dead. And, in a way, it was better that they didn't.

The dead could help.

But the Krewe also needed help from the living.

"There was...something," she whispered.

"In the morgue?"

"I couldn't *really* feel her. I didn't sense her moving around or even see her. But I could tell that she was still here. Does that make sense? And I keep seeing her on Bourbon Street. In my dreams. She's walking toward me. And there's something behind me. Something black and malignant." She shuddered.

Halloween. Only five nights away now.

Jake wondered why he felt that if they could just make it through Halloween, everything would be all right.

Jackson was quiet. He had taken the back seat, allowing Ashley the front, while Jake drove.

"Jackson?" Jake asked.

"Who knows, Ashley?" Jackson said. "We never really have answers. Maybe you met her somewhere years ago, brushed by her in the street. Maybe she came out to Donegal Plantation with a school group or something. But somehow, I believe, she's a very lost, scared, and desperate ghost. And so she's coming to you in your dreams. For help."

"Maybe we should stage something," Jake said thoughtfully.

"Stage something?" Ashley asked. "Like what? We already have some staged scenes going on—pretty gruesome stuff. What do you mean exactly?"

"I'm not sure yet—after we meet your scare cast, I may have a better idea of what is swirling around in my head," Jake told her.

He met Jackson's eyes in the rearview mirror.

Jackson, he thought, was thinking along similar lines.

* * * *

It had to be the art studio people who were evil, Ashley thought. *Not* someone connected to Donegal Plantation.

Beth was great at hiring people. She would have checked out backgrounds on anyone she brought onto the property. And her grandfather was no fool. No one was ever hired without Beth, Frazier, and Cliff all agreeing that they were right for the job.

Of course, some people were known criminals. They couldn't be caught or prosecuted for some crimes, but they might have records for the minor infractions that prosecutors had been able to prove in court.

Unfortunately, some people did get away with crimes.

Including murder.

But this was vigilantism. And when it became this broad, the criminals would make mistakes.

Just like this trio had.

They'd killed an innocent girl. And they'd killed another thug—but in front of witnesses. They were being found out.

Still...

Beth was sitting on the porch, a notebook in her hands, when they arrived.

She immediately hopped up, happy to welcome Jackson—but then became suspicious. Jackson wasn't supposed to be here.

She was quick, though, and put things together. "This has something to do with the murders in New Orleans, doesn't it?" she asked.

"Yep," Jackson told her. "Weird enough for the Krewe—I'm sure you've seen the news. Witches. And we've been asked to help."

"Figured that was what Jake was up to," Beth said. "Great wedding planning," she added dryly, looking at Ashley.

"There's nothing to worry about. You and Frazier will know what we're doing. All we have to do is wait for the ghosts and ghoulies and spiders and all to come down...and some pretty stuff to go up. We've really got it all under control. And besides, it's almost Halloween. So it will all be over in a few days, no matter what." Ashley looked around. "Where are all our actors?"

"Getting set for tonight," Beth said, looking at her watch. "Gates open to the public in about an hour."

"Want to meet the cast?" Ashley asked Jake and Jackson.

Beth wasn't fooled. "Good Lord, please tell me that this isn't going to... Oh, no. Donegal is involved somehow?"

"No," Jake said.

"I think you're lying, *special agent*," Beth accused.

Jackson told her, "Honestly, Donegal isn't involved. Not in the way you're thinking. We just want to talk to one of your cast members. He knew the young woman who was murdered."

"What is the world coming to?" Beth muttered. "That's something I've asked myself more and more over the last few years." She pointed down to the outbuildings. "Go, children, save the world. Or, at the least, some hapless souls in the state of Louisiana. And quite frankly, you all should stay to see what's going on here—and let us know if we need to stop."

"You haven't had anything bad happen here, have you?" Jake asked.

"Lots of screaming. But all in fun," Beth said.

"This way," Ashley told the two of them.

She headed first for the smokehouse—and Jonathan Starling. After all, he'd known Shelley Broussard.

Jake and Jackson trailed behind her. She opened the door. For a moment, she wondered if she should have knocked—he was the only actor working in the smokehouse.

But it was her property. Her smokehouse. And he was, at this time and place, her employee.

"Hey, there," she said.

He was adjusting some of his props. The lights were all on and there was also a bit of sunlight still coming through the cracks in the paper covering the windows.

"Hey, yourself." He smiled. He wasn't dressed for the night yet. Then again, his costume was just something of a butcher's coat—covered in blood. "I heard you were going to be here tonight. I'm awfully glad. We really hope that we're pleasing you."

"Body parts, blood, screaming... Halloween. What's not to like?" Ashley joked.

"I love working out here," he said. "Some of the guys are from Baton Rouge. I'm from NOLA. I'm—I'm glad to be out of the city."

She didn't reply as Jake and Jackson walked in behind her.

"This is pretty cool," Jake said, looking around the room.

"Definitely frightening," Jackson agreed.

"Jonathan, this is my fiancé, Jake Mallory. And Jackson Crow, head of Jake's unit."

"Unit. Oh, yeah, I heard you were FBI," Jonathan said, looking from Jake to Jackson. He smiled ruefully then. "You're not just here because...because you kind of live here," he said to Jake. "You're both here because of Shelley."

"Yes," Jake said flatly. There was no other reply. "You did know her. How well? And why did they think you two were arguing at the art shop?"

"I didn't want her there," he said softly.

"There—at the art shop?" Jackson asked him.

Jonathan nodded gravely. "There was something—wrong with it all. I mean, Nick Nicholson acts all noble—like he's a great patron of the arts. But there was something weird about the situation. Shelley would break appointments with me because of these 'meetings' they were going to have. What was there to meet about?" He frowned, seeming to be reliving the discussion in his mind. "They took turns being clerks. When they were off, they could still go hang stuff up at Jackson Square. But..."

"You were angry because of the meetings?" Ashley asked.

"Because it wasn't right. The whole thing wasn't right. It was just creepy."

"Why didn't you come forward when she was killed?" Jake asked him.

He lifted his hands. "Come forward with what? It was no secret that I was seeing her—though she pushed me out of the shop often enough. It was as if... If she had a boyfriend, she couldn't be there. Does that make sense to you? That was how she acted. And I tried to tell her that if it was all above board and normal, having a boyfriend wouldn't matter at all. It wouldn't mean anything. Most young women have boyfriends."

"Did you ever see or hear of them doing anything...not right?" Jackson asked.

"No," Jonathan admitted grudgingly. "Just...those meetings. And making it such a special thing for a young woman to be named one of their shop artists. You didn't see any men there, did you?"

Jake and Jackson seldom betrayed what they were thinking and they didn't now.

"When did you last see her?"

"The day before she was killed. We were supposed to go out the following morning. I was already working here, so my nights were taken. She called me and said that she was having another of her meetings, but maybe we could get together when it was over. I told her that if the meetings were more important than me, she shouldn't worry about it. We were over. Then... Then I learned through the news that she was dead." His voice was tremulous. He looked at Ashley suddenly. "That's why I'm so damned glad I'm out here. Out here... I'm not even going back to NOLA at night. I—I can't go back there. Not now."

The door opened. Parks had arrived.

"This is Detective Parks with NOPD," Jake told Jonathan.

"How do you do, sir?" Jonathan said.

"I don't know. How do I do?" Parks asked, looking at them one by one.

"Jonathan thinks that there's something up with the art shop," Jake said.

Parks nodded. "So much for casual, huh?" he asked.

"What?" Jonathan asked, confused.

"Not to worry," Ashley said. "I'm going to take them to meet our witches."

"Our witches haven't been killing anyone," Jonathan said.

"And how do you know that?" Parks asked.

"They didn't kill Shelley," Jonathan said, and his voice was thin. "They were here that night, scaring the bejesus out of those unwary souls who walked into the gingerbread house."

"What time do you close?" Detective Parks asked.

"Our last groups go through the kitchen, the smokehouse, and do the haunted hayride at midnight. But after, it's not always easy to get people out. After they're all gone, we do some cleaning up. So we're out of here between 1:00 and 2:00 A.M."

"She could have been left there any time, son," Parks told him. "She was killed elsewhere and brought to the wall of the cemetery."

Jonathan looked sick, as if he might just break down and cry. "I didn't kill her, I swear. I loved her." He stared at Jake suddenly. "I loved her. Look into that art studio—something is wrong."

"Are you all right?" Ashley asked him. "Jonathan, do you need someone to take your place tonight?"

He shook his head. "Work," he said huskily. "Work—keeps me sane."

"Thank you, Jonathan," Jackson said. "And if you think of anything—"

Jackson, Jake, and Detective Parks all handed him their business cards.

"Call any one of us," Jake told him.

Jonathan nodded glumly, staring into space. "I loved her," he repeated. "I really loved her. I just couldn't compete with…with whatever it was."

Chapter 10

Witches.

At first, they'd been looking for witches.

Then it became clowns.

But the truth was, it was neither.

It was three chameleon-like killers who didn't want to be caught and who—it seemed—were so adept at their costume changes that they were doing quite well.

Meeting Ashley's "witches," Jake couldn't begin to think of any of them as cold-blooded killers.

The actresses playing in the gingerbread house were Lavinia Carole, Valerie Deering, and Rhonda Blackstone. They all smiled genuinely when they met Jake, Jackson, and Parks—as if they were truly innocent of even being aware of any wrongdoing, much less a part of it.

"Jake. Fiancé Jake, right?" Lavinia asked. "We've heard people say that Ashley's fiancé was…um, big."

Valerie laughed. "Handsome is what we've heard," she said.

"And you're an agent, too?" Rhonda asked Jackson.

"He's actually my boss," Jake told her.

"Oh, nice," Lavinia said. "And you, sir?" She turned to Parks.

"NOPD," Parks said.

"Oh, are you the officer on duty here tonight?" Rhonda asked.

"I'm on duty, but there will also be a man in uniform here, like always," Parks said.

"I was about to practice being pushed into the oven. Want to see how it works?" Lavinia asked them. "One of you has to be an attendee," she warned.

"Ashley—you be the evil child who cooks the witch," Jake suggested.

She made a face at him, but complied.

The witches had a good act. They went right into cackling and running around for their spices, talking about the delicious children they would serve up. Or, if there were no children, an adult would do just fine. Nothing like a little NOLA spice on their meals, huh? Where was the hot sauce?

Then Lavinia began circling Ashley, smiling and speaking sweetly while apparently mentally chopping her up into meal-sized portions.

It became obvious that Ashley would need to shut Lavinia into the "oven" if she didn't want to be staying for dinner.

So Ashley did.

Lavinia screamed and cooked while her "sisters" wailed.

Parks clapped. "Excellent job."

"Yes, and if this were real, one of our ghostly escorts would move people on over to the smokehouse and then to the haunted hayride. As soon as they're out of here—before the next group gets in—Lavinia just comes back in. It's fun and we have a great time doing it."

They talked a few minutes more, laughing and chatting casually.

"Do you go home every night—back to New Orleans?" Jake asked.

"Well, I'm from Biloxi," Lavinia said.

"I'm actually from Slidell," Rhonda told them.

"I'm a NOLA girl," Valerie added.

"But," Lavinia said, "we haven't been going home. My aunt has a place just up the road. She's alone a lot—my uncle is military—so she's been happy to have all three of us."

"Nice," Jackson told her. "You need to stay together, and be careful," he added.

"We don't go many places these days—we head from my aunt's house to here, and when we're finished for the night, we go right back," Valerie said.

"Yeah. It's a scary world out there," Lavinia agreed. "And that has nothing to do with Halloween."

"Too true. And I'm glad you're being safe. Continue to be smart and careful," Detective Parks said.

They all exited the old kitchen.

Parks sighed. "Well, I'm glad. Even though this has cost us all an afternoon, none of your people so far seem to fit the trio we're looking for. But you have more of the horror-house-actors, or whatever they're called, right?" He turned to Ashley.

"All over Louisiana—and the country—you'll find scare actors at this time of the year," Ashley said.

"If only it were all acting." Parks shook his head.

"Come on," Ashley said quietly. "The others must all be out by the haunted hayride. There wasn't anyone else on the porch with Beth earlier."

"Where's your grandfather?" Jake asked. He realized he sounded worried. But he was. It just wasn't a good situation.

He used to love Halloween.

This Halloween, however…

Witches. Clowns.

"He's most likely in his study. We'll see him before we all take off—okay?"

"I would love to see your grandfather," Parks told Ashley.

"Shall we move on?" Jake asked.

As Ashley had expected, the others *were* out by the hay wagon, helping to spruce it up for the night and chatting. Cliff was there, directing everyone. While they hired actors to work the "scares" on the hayride, Cliff drove the wagon.

No one else worked with Donegal horses.

"Ashley," Cliff called, always pleased to see her. But he frowned when he saw Jake and the others. "And Jake, hey. Jackson Crow, I'll be damned, you're back here?" He chuckled. "The wedding isn't for another month. And hello, sir." He raised his eyebrows.

"Detective Parks, a friend from NOLA, Cliff," Ashley said quickly. "Just showing them all the activity going on."

Cliff glanced around as he hauled a cushion up to go beneath some fresh hay. Apparently satisfied that Jackson and Parks were far enough away, he spoke softly, so that only Ashley and Jake could hear.

"Yeah?" he murmured. "Like hell. Jake's working the NOLA murders."

"Yep."

He turned to the staff, a big smile on his face. "Hear ye, hear ye, Donegal ghosts and ghoulies. Meet some friends of the family. Jake Mallory, Ashley's fiancé, Jackson Crow, friend to all, and another friend—"

He broke off. He'd never met Isaac Parks.

"And Isaac Parks," Ashley finished, as if stepping in on him.

"We're the ghosts," Artie Lane said, stepping up to shake hands with Jake, Jackson, and the detective. "Although," he added with a dry grin, "the plantation is supposed to actually be haunted."

"Trina DeMoine," Trina said, introducing herself. "And what respectable plantation isn't haunted?"

"Shy ghosts," Harold Corn said, coming up as well. "So we kind of materialize for them. I'm Harold, and that pretty woman over there is Sandy Patterson. We have stations on the property where we pop up and follow the wagon and do cute ghost tricks while Cliff tells a few wild tales."

"And we're guides," Alex Maple announced, coming up to introduce himself as well. "Bill Davis is the tall, skinny guy there, and Jerry Harte rounds out our group. We keep people moving. Three groups are out at any time. One in the gingerbread house, one in the old smokehouse, and one on the hayride. Beth wrangles the groups on the porch—we keep each down to twenty people. It's a lot more fun that way for those coming in, and we stay fairly sane."

"Sounds good," Jake said. "Any trouble out here lately?"

Bill Davis came forward, frowning. "Should we be worried?"

"No, not about anything that we know in particular. Careful, yes," Jake said. "There are always some true monsters running around at Halloween."

"We have a cop," Trina said.

"And security. They won't get here for about another half hour or so—just before the gates are open to the public," Alex told them. "They're good—we have to be careful sometimes not to touch or be touched, but even then... No real trouble. Alcohol isn't allowed here—even when people are done. It's just tea and whatever's on the porch. No one gets too feisty."

"He's not talking about feisty guests," Bill said, studying the trio of lawmen. He pointed at Isaac Parks. "You're the detective on the murder case in New Orleans. Cases, I should say. We were just comparing them. Discussing what's been going on in the news."

"Some vigilantes have been killing bad guys," Artie said. "We're not bad guys, so I think we're okay."

"They killed a very sweet young woman too, we believe," Parks said.

"You don't know that," Trina said. "Really, I can't see the correlation—why would the police even think that? And I don't know—all those bad guys down. Whoever these vigilantes are, they might be on the right path. Hey, that guy—that Tink guy they killed—he was a major cocaine and heroin dealer and he was suspected of killing a bunch of people. Okay, maybe they were bad people too, but—"

"We have laws for a reason," Jake said quietly. "And courts—for a reason. Judges to dole out punishment. We prove guilt—we don't assume it. Part and parcel of being American."

"But seriously..." Harold began.

"Yes, seriously. We have courts. A system. Laws. Not only is being judge and jury all in one illegal, but the wrong people wind up hurt," Jake said. He felt himself growing angry.

He couldn't get Shelley Broussard out of his mind.

"But sometimes..." Trina said, and then paused, shrugging. "Forgive me. Sometimes, the courts aren't so effective. But to answer your question, no—we haven't had any trouble out here. And—" She looked at Ashley and smiled. "We're an hour out of the city of New Orleans. People looking for trouble... They don't usually want to drive this far to find it."

"But we're careful," Harold added. "We watch." He looked at Ashley. "And, I swear, we would report anything immediately. You know that."

"I do," Ashley said. "Seriously, these guys just wanted to see what was going on out here. Fun, huh?"

"Well, we were having fun," Harold said.

"Go back to your fun—sorry. We didn't mean to be a damper," Jake said. "Just be careful—and alert. Even if it is Halloween."

"Of course."

"Sure."

"You bet."

The group all spoke in unison.

"Let's finish this up," Cliff said.

"Yep, see you all later," Ashley called out cheerfully.

She walked ahead of Jake. He caught up to her, slipping an arm around her shoulders.

"Jake," she murmured.

"Sorry. This is just..."

"Halloween," she said.

"Let's see your grandfather, all right?"

She glanced at him. "Shouldn't you be back in New Orleans?"

"Not tonight," he told her. "Not tonight."

* * * *

Jake was worried, Ashley knew.

She was worried herself.

Frazier was just fine, hiding in his study. He told them both he'd be there all night. That he would, in fact, be in his study—unless he was in the dining room or upstairs in his bed—until Halloween was over.

Jackson and Parks went back to New Orleans.

Parks was going to get a man to take over for Jude McCoy, who'd been watching over Richard Showalter. Then Jackson and Jude intended to keep a good eye on the art studio and follow Nick Nicholson if and when he headed out.

Parks himself was going to walk Bourbon Street.

"You should really be in NOLA," Ashley told Jake at one point.

But Jake was stubborn. That night, at least, he was going to be at Donegal Plantation. With her.

Naturally, they were booked to the gills. There was no way for her or Jake to take a customer's place in the house tours or on the hayride. But they tried their best to keep an eye on the groups.

The security company people walked around just as they should.

Their cop stayed on duty.

No one was even slightly feisty.

The night came and went.

Jake kept in close contact with Parks and Jackson and Jude McCoy.

But nothing happened in the city of New Orleans either.

A quiet night.

And still.

Once she fell asleep, Ashley dreamed. She heard the sound of music blaring, louder and louder from each consecutive bar and club. She saw the neon lights and heard the laughter of the people on Bourbon Street.

And ahead of her was the young woman.

Shelley Broussard.

"Help me, please," Shelley whispered.

Ashley didn't need to turn to see that the black mist, the cloud of birds, ebony evil, or whatever it might be, was coming.

"No," Ashley begged. "Please help me, Shelley. I need your help so badly."

Shelley stopped. "I am Shelley Broussard," she said. "And I am dead. They murdered me."

"Help me," Ashley pleaded.

"Yes… I know. I am Shelley Broussard. And I am dead. And… I want to help you."

She disappeared.

The black mist was coming.

Ashley almost felt it.

It was cold and had a horrible feel. Slimy, and somehow as evil as the menace it promised.

Cold…like death.

Ashley woke with a start. Jake was holding her, rocking with her.

And in his arms, she felt the cold burn away, and his warmth engulf her.

Chapter 11

"Shelley's body hasn't been released to the family—or to Marty and Nick Nicholson," Jake said, pacing the floor in the bedroom. He stopped and stared at Ashley. "So, yes. It's still possible to see her. To touch her."

"I just feel that if…if I get a real chance, I'll be able to communicate with her," Ashley said. "And even if she can't tell me who killed her, if they came at her from behind and she couldn't see them—she might be able to tell me more about Jonathan Starling. We can find out if he is sincere. Or if the people at the art gallery really are practicing some kind of weird murder rituals—and Shelley just wound up in the way. I'm just afraid that if we ask to see her body again, they're going to think we're stark-raving mad."

"No, it's all right," Jake said, waving a hand in the air. "Jude McCoy was with the NOLA office before he was with the Krewe—he's good at dealing with Orleans Parish and the M.E.s here. We'll be fine." He offered her a lopsided smile. "Hey, we're the Krewe of Hunters. We believe in…whatever needs to be believed in."

"Thankfully. But shouldn't you be in New Orleans? You know I really need to stay out here. The next five nights will be hard for everyone because it's the end of the season. I mean, I want to go into New Orleans and back to the morgue, but after that, I need to be home. Still, as far as you going back…"

"Parks is a good detective. He's had his men out and watching Picture This, and Nick and Marty Nicholson and the young artists working at the shop. They've all been quiet. Either cops or FBI have followed them all and they've done nothing but eat, buy supplies—and deliver paintings. Oh, the woman you met at Jackson Square—

Geraldine Sands—has moved in. Jackson was by there and met her. She said that she has your painting and she can arrange to have it delivered or we can pick it up."

"It's a nice painting," Ashley told him. "Not quite as haunting as the one I bought by Shelley."

"Hmm. And you just had to wear the costume that made you appear to be the same person—*hauntingly* brought back to life?" he queried.

"She calls to me, Jake," Ashley told him softly.

He inclined his head, and then nodded. "All right. We'll get to the morgue. And then we'll get you back here." He hesitated, shaking his head. "I don't like it. I just don't like it."

"What?"

"Halloween. Even here in this place, when it's open to the public," he murmured.

"We know everyone working here—and costumes other than on our actors are not allowed. We have a security company and a cop. And we have Cliff, and—trust me—Frazier knows how to use his double-barreled shotgun."

"I know. Still… He might just be a damned good liar. But Jonathan Starling remains a person of interest, you know."

"He's one man. And there are three killers."

"You have three witches working your gingerbread house."

"That would equal four."

"There could be one mastermind—and three carrying out the plans," Jake said. "That would be four."

"Go to work, Jake. Don't worry so much about me. Nothing has happened out here. I mean, first take me to the morgue. Then go to work."

He nodded. "Think we'll actually make it to a wedding?" he asked her.

She nodded. "And a honeymoon."

He grinned at that and put through a call to Jackson. They drove back into the city.

The same M.E. met them and watched curiously as they studied the body. It was just Jake and Ashley this time. Jake questioned the M.E. a bit, trying to distract her so that Ashley could get closer.

Shelley remained very cold. Icy to the touch. Ashley closed her eyes.

"I'm here. I feel you. Shelley, please let me help you."

The corpse remained cold. Jake continued to speak with the medical examiner. They left a few minutes later.

"Anything?" Jake asked when they were outside.

"I know she's here—somewhere," Ashley said softly. "I don't understand why I can't see her, hear her, when I'm awake. I know it's her, and I'm getting closer to her in my dreams."

Jake's phone rang as she was speaking and he excused himself to answer it. She watched his face grow grim as he listened.

"That was Jackson," he told her briefly. "I'm going to head out to Baton Rouge with Jude. The police there spoke with Angela, and they started to draw up a few of their own comparisons. These people might have been busy for a long time in Louisiana. We're trying to work up a timeline—when people could have been where."

"Jonathan Starling pointed out that *our* witches were working when Shelley was killed."

"Maybe—and maybe not. Shelley Broussard's body was set up. But still, she was dumped. She was killed elsewhere. And the M.E. can't really pinpoint time of death."

"Jake, with everything that Angela discovered... And if the Baton Rouge police are right and anything they have corresponds with these killings, this trio might have been at this a very long time. There—there may be no solution here—even if the art shop is watched every day. Even if Jonathan Starling is in some way guilty of something."

"No. They're making mistakes. And we'll catch them."

A car pulled up and Jackson stepped out of it. Jude, who was driving, waved to Ashley. She waved back. Jake gave her a quick kiss on the cheek. "Jackson will be with you. He's going to work at the plantation and..."

"And he'll be there, watching over me, through all the Halloween shenanigans of the night," Ashley finished.

"Precisely," he said.

"Go," Ashley directed. She smiled and he went out to join Jude.

Jackson walked up to her, carrying his computer case. "Seems like you get me for the evening. Sorry."

She smiled at him. "I never mind having you for the evening. In fact, I'm honored. I'm being watched over by the best there is."

"I'm sure that's debatable," he said. "But, onward. How did the morning go? Am I driving or are you?"

Ashley opted to drive. And as she did so, they spoke about the case. "The thing is, I don't think that the killers knew most of their victims in any way, shape, or form. Except for Shelley. Then why are they associated? I mean, would vigilantes kill a girl so sweet and innocent?"

"The greater good," Jackson said.

"The greater good?"

"If they felt that they were on an important mission, then maybe. Also, there's another possibility."

"What's that?"

"Someone is so full of their own ego that it just doesn't matter. If you can touch her... If you can find out what she felt or believed regarding people, it would definitely help."

Soon enough, they reached Donegal.

Donegal, decked out in black drapes, spiders here and there, ghosts and goblins hanging about the porch.

Jackson told her he was going to head out and make sure that everyone was where they should be—and that it was the right people in the right place for Donegal in the evening.

Ashley found her grandfather in his study, seated at his desk. She walked behind him and slipped her arms around his neck. He patted her hand. "You stay up by the house tonight, you hear?" he asked.

"I'll stay up by the house," she promised.

"I'm imagining it now," he said. "Lilies, gardenias, magnolias...white and light. And you and me walking down that stairway, Jake and his men coming from the other side, everything beautiful. The best of it all being that you've found the right young man—you're going to lead a good life. Okay, a crazy life, but...with a good man. It'll be a good life. And eventually, there will be little feet running up and down the stairways again."

She smiled. Frazier was definitely ready for great-grandchildren.

"Little footsteps," she said.

"Of course, these days, there could have been little footsteps already. But though I am anxious—and you two did take forever—I like the order we're working in. Wedding, and then children."

"Glad to please," Ashley said lightly. "I'm going to go up and change into something 1860s so that I can help Beth wrangle our haunted-house-goers."

"I shall be here—far from the cackling witches and madmen or whoever else you have out there," he told her. "I'm looking at taking in a rescue horse from the Florida panhandle. Poor thing. No brand, just wandering off I-10. Call me if you need me."

"Will do," Ashley promised him.

The grand foyer was empty. If she wasn't quite so caught up in what was happening, she would be marveling more about her own upcoming wedding.

But that time would come.

And she did have Beth and Cliff, and her amazing grandfather, and all kinds of people who would help, who would be there.

She hurried upstairs and went for the costume she used during re-enactments.

But chose not to use it. Standing in her underwear, she found herself staring at Shelley's painting.

As she watched it, the character in the painting seemed to move. To reach out. The eyes grew even larger...

"Shelley, damn you, speak to me," she said.

"I'm—I'm here."

She turned.

At last, a very pale image of the woman she knew through the painting, through her dreams—and through the morgue—appeared. She stood just inside the French doors to the wraparound balcony like she was created of just a bit of substance and light from the day's dying sun.

But she was there.

"Shelley," Ashley breathed.

"Help me," Shelley whispered. "Lord, I'm praying I can...can help you help me."

* * * *

"I wound up talking to Nate Gallen, one of our patrol officers," Captain Raoul Peterson told Jake and Jude. They'd easily made their way to Baton Rouge and were discussing the case in the captain's office. "He's not a detective, but he was first on the scene. It wasn't quite a month ago. October 1st, to be exact. Gallen came upon a murder. Terrible site, blood everywhere. And when he reported to me, he told me that he saw ghosts leaving the scene. So naturally, he took a lot of ribbings. Whoever the murderer was, the victim was one slippery eel. He'd just gotten let out on a murder charge himself. I remember the case. Judge declared the evidence against him was 'fruit of the poisonous tree,' something about a warrant not being right. Anyway, the dead man had supposedly left a few dead men behind. But we didn't have evidence—except for that obtained before a search warrant was granted. Thing is, my officer swore that he saw three ghosts. Even when his buddies all teased the bloody hell out of him. And it wasn't the ghosts that got to me so much. It was the fact that he'd seen *three* of them."

Jake glanced at Jude.

Ghosts. Three of them.

"Anyway, I have the case files in hard copy there for you, and we can email anything else that you may want as well," the captain said. "It sounds like they're out of our jurisdiction now, and I can't believe I'm saying this, but I hope to hell you get those ghosts. Oh, and one more thing."

"What's that?"

"Well, my officer was babbling. That's why no one took him seriously. But he was babbling about Halloween. About Halloween night being some kind of a grand finale to what the ghosts did."

"Can we see him?" Jake asked.

"Poor fellow—we had to put him on leave. Doctors have him somewhere in Montana right now. I can arrange it, if you like."

Jake's phone buzzed. "Excuse me," he murmured. He didn't recognize the number.

"Special Agent Mallory," he said.

"Mallory, Jake... You gave me your card. This is Richard Showalter."

Jake could barely hear, since the man was almost whispering.

"Yes, what is it? What's happened?"

"There was supposed to be an officer watching me. He...he's not here. He was here. He went out to check on a noise... And he's gone."

"All right, stay calm. I'm a distance away. I'm having Detective Parks get someone there right away. Are you inside? Is the alarm on?"

There was no answer.

"Captain, thank you," Jake said, rising. Jude did the same. They both shook hands with the captain and Jake led them out at double speed.

"What's going on?" Jude asked.

"That was Richard Showalter. He can't find his cop."

"He might be doing rounds."

"Showalter's phone cut out."

Jude swore softly.

As they headed to the car, Jake called Parks, and then Jackson.

And they drove like hell toward New Orleans.

* * * *

"Why were you labeled a traitor? Who did this to you?" Ashley asked.

Shelley smiled sweetly. "I don't know."

"I know your killer came up from behind, but... Why a traitor?"

"I didn't want to be involved."

"In what?"

Shelley waved a hand in the air. "Whatever it was that they were doing. We'd have all these ridiculous meetings—as if we were back in high school trying to pledge for some kind of a club. I wanted to do other things. I didn't want to be a part of them." She closed her eyes. "I guess that means they killed me."

"They?"

"And the other two, Samantha Perkins and Emily Dupont. They told me they were part of the League of Reformation, and that I needed to be one of them. And to do that, I had to learn to behave and obey. I laughed them off a few times. I got angry a few times."

Ashley's phone started ringing. She dug in her pocket for it. As she did so, the image of Shelley began to fade away. "No, no, no," Ashley said.

But Shelley was gone.

She answered the phone.

It was Beth. "Come on down. The gates are open. You're helping out tonight, right?"

"Yes, on my way."

She silently swore as she dressed hastily—in the witch costume—and hurried downstairs. She'd had Shelley with her. She was so close. And now she knew. She knew that the girls that Shelley had lived with were in on her murder. She called Jake as quickly as she could, heading down the stairs.

"Jake, I saw her—I saw Shelley. And the women she lived with are in on it. I think that makes Nick Nicholson the head of it all."

"I'll have them picked up. Right now... Right now we have a cop down. He isn't dead. He was guarding Richard Showalter."

"Is Showalter dead?"

"We don't know. He's gone. There's a lot of blood. We—we don't know if it's his blood mixed in there or not. Ashley, be careful. Don't leave the property."

"I won't," she promised.

She reached the porch and quickly joined Beth in handing out little paper bracelets, colored for time and place on the haunted tour of the property.

But then she looked up.

And saw Shelley Broussard.

Walking toward the family graveyard.

"Sorry, be right back," she promised Beth.

And she hurried after the ghost, forgetting that she looked exactly like the dead girl herself.

* * * *

They were nearing the plantation when Jake saw that Parks was calling him.

He answered.

"We picked up the girls," Parks said. "And Marty Nicholson."

"What about Nicholson himself?" Jake asked.

"I don't think he was part of it."

"Why not?"

"Because he's dead. His throat was slit."

* * * *

"You didn't tell her that we're on our way to Donegal," Jude noted.

"You don't know Ashley," Jake said, shaking his head. "I'd hear about her being fine, and that I should be going where I was needed. This way, there's no argument. I'll just go there. And..." He paused.

Jude looked at him. "And?"

"Parks and the police are covering New Orleans right now—including anything to do with Showalter's house and the injured detective. Maybe these killers are getting better at watching out for decent targets. We need to be at Donegal Plantation."

"Why?"

"Because Ashley knows that the girls living with Shelley were involved. There are two of your witches."

"So that's it—two witches?"

Jake shook his head. "No, three witches—and some sort of a commander, priest, evil god—a man."

"Okay, so Nick and Marty Nicholson."

"Marty, yes. She's the third witch."

"And Nick?"

"Could be, though I doubt they killed their leader."

"It could be someone else. Thing is, Parks has to get those women behind bars. Tonight. Quickly."

* * * *

The graveyard at Donegal Plantation was truly beautiful. A collection of funerary art, it covered mid-nineteenth century to the present. The Donegal family tomb was most grand, offering up angels and cherubs and gargoyles.

The ghost walked right through the gate and the wall that surrounded the cemetery.

Ashley had to unlatch the gate—she was afraid of hurting herself with a leap over the little wall in her elaborate dress.

"Shelley, wait."

But as she walked in, she saw that the ghost of Shelley was crying out and running.

And as she chased after Shelley, Ashley realized that someone was chasing after her.

Jonathan Starling.

Shelley was running, but...

Did Starling see the ghost?

Or was he running after her?

Ashley's heart began to thud.

Jake had been afraid for her, angry because of this very costume. And now this man who had harassed Shelley, who had claimed to love her, was chasing her.

Ashley turned back. He was wearing his bloodied costume and carrying a meat cleaver.

She hopped over an in-ground stone and swung around a cherub before she was able to dive behind the Donegal family tomb. She saw an old brick that had fallen free from a planter and snatched it up quickly.

When Jonathan Starling came around the tomb, she raised the stone high. And as she did, she remembered that she had clocked Cliff once long ago—afraid that he was a killer.

She struck.

Jonathan fell.

And the ghost of Shelley Broussard appeared.

"No, no, not Jonathan. Never Jonathan. He loved me. I love him."

"Then?" Ashley whispered the word.

"Miss Donegal, I'm so sorry. So, so, sorry that you can't let things go."

She turned.

And found Richard Showalter stalking her way.

He was alone, she saw. He hadn't slit anyone's throat—he'd had his followers do it for him.

But that didn't matter.

He was a killer, through and through.

"You are truly an idiot," Ashley said. She was far enough away, and the brick was still in her hand. "You'll definitely be caught now. You're going to try to murder me—on my own property? Tonight?"

"You're a meddler. And a traitor to good. You have to die."

"I'm a traitor? Because I want to stop you?"

"I have been working for justice. You are a traitor to justice. Happy to let killers walk. I hunt down monsters."

"You killed Shelley."

"Shelley was a traitor."

"You can't just kill people."

He continued walking toward her, smiling. "You're going to hit me with that brick?"

"You're a hypocrite," she told him. "You're the monster."

Closer, closer. She kept her eyes on him while she spoke.

"What did you do to get here? Kill a cop? The clowns weren't coming after you to kill you—they were coming for instructions. Richard Showalter," she sneered. "Known for his work against vigilantism. You hypocritical bastard. And you killed Shelley. Killed Shelley because she wouldn't become part of your killing machine.

You—God… You're absolutely a monster."

"And you're absolutely dead."

The closer he came, the greater the terror that filled her. She saw what he carried.

He hadn't killed before. But he planned to kill now. He had an ice pick. If he was able to get in just one good blow…

Suddenly, the ghost of Shelley Broussard raced out, a cry of fury on her lips.

The man paused, blinking. As if fog had gotten in his eyes, as if he'd seen something but didn't understand what.

He staggered, coming toward Ashley. She raised her brick and bashed him.

He caught her arm.

She screamed.

And even as the sound left her lips, Jake was there. Pulling the man from her, throwing him to the ground. And Jackson was behind Jake, ready to wrench him up and handcuff him.

But as she rushed into Jake's arms, she dimly realized that Jackson wasn't arresting him. Parks had arrived and was angrily reading Richard Showalter his rights.

"You nearly killed my man—a good man!" Parks roared.

"He killed Shelley," Ashley said, staring at Jake. "He killed Shelley. Whether he drew the blade or not and— We have to get an ambulance. Jonathan Starling came out here and…"

"And you clocked him?" he asked, but pointed to Jackson, who was already helping a dazed Jonathan.

Jake was smiling, but his eyes were filled with concern, and she felt him shaking.

He loved her so much.

As she loved him.

"You do seem to like to clock the wrong people," Jake said and tightened his hold. "What am I going to do with you? I have to keep you out of danger."

"Well, you are marrying me, of course."

"Not so sure that's really going to help," he teased.

And then he kissed her.

* * * *

In the days that followed, the horror of what had been going on for weeks began to become clear.

Nick Nicholson had really just been a nice guy—trying to help artists. He hadn't known that his wife started out having an affair with Richard Showalter—only to become so infatuated with him that she more or less became the mother for his cult of monsters recruited to kill monsters. He thought himself a genius. Use monsters at Halloween. Who would notice?

But Shelley Broussard could not be coerced, brainwashed, or convinced in any way. And with the rest of the women in the household killing, she had to play a part.

Or disappear.

Ashley spent time with Jonathan Starling and hoped he was really going to be all right.

He had seen or sensed something about Shelley. And the day after Halloween, when the cast came to help clean out and pick up their own belongings, she saw him in the cemetery. And she saw Shelley sitting next to him.

Then Shelley was gone.

Ashley went to talk to him. Tears streamed down his cheeks. "She told me I must move on," he said. He looked at her. "I saw her. I really saw her."

"I believe you. And I believe that she's moved on now—and that means that you must, too. You must move on."

They sat together for a while.

And then she went back to the house, where Frazier, Beth, Cliff, and Jake were all debating if they should wait, if Ashley was all right with what had happened.

"I'm getting married right here. In two weeks," Ashley said. She saw Jake smile, and that was all she needed.

And, two weeks later, they were back.

The spiders were gone, along with the black draping, the ghosts, the demons, and all else that had been part of Halloween.

Flowers were everywhere.

The plantation had never looked more spectacular.

Most of the Krewe were in attendance. Jackson and Angela, and Whitney and Kat and Will and so many others.

It was splendid. Frazier was dignified, and he cried when he had to give a speech at the reception. She and Jake caught him in a sandwich hug, and she gave a speech back, thanking him for being the best grandparent ever.

And that night...

Well, the grounds thronged with Krewe. While the honeymoon beckoned come morning, for the night...

They would never find a place so safe to abandon all and make love.

And make love.

Again, and again, and again.

Even a lifetime might not be enough. Then again...

It seemed that love could last forever, far longer than a lifetime.

* * * *

Also from 1001 Dark Nights and Heather Graham, discover Crimson Twilight, When Irish Eyes Are Haunting, All Hallow's Eve, and Blood on the Bayou.

Sign up for the 1001 Dark Nights Newsletter
and be entered to win a Tiffany Key necklace.

There's a contest every month!

Go to www.1001DarkNights.com to subscribe.

As a bonus, all subscribers will receive a free
1001 Dark Nights story
The First Night
by Lexi Blake & M.J. Rose

Turn the page for a full list of the
1001 Dark Nights fabulous novellas...

Discover 1001 Dark Nights Collection Four
Go to www.1001DarkNights.com to subscribe.

ROCK CHICK REAWAKENING by Kristen Ashley
A Rock Chick Novella

ADORING INK by Carrie Ann Ryan
A Montgomery Ink Novella

SWEET RIVALRY by K. Bromberg

SHADE'S LADY by Joanna Wylde
A Reapers MC Novella

RAZR by Larissa Ione
A Demonica Underworld Novella

ARRANGED by Lexi Blake
A Masters and Mercenaries Novella

TANGLED by Rebecca Zanetti
A Dark Protectors Novella

HOLD ME by J. Kenner
A Stark Ever After Novella

SOMEHOW, SOME WAY by Jennifer Probst
A Billionaire Builders Novella

TOO CLOSE TO CALL by Tessa Bailey
A Romancing the Clarksons Novella

HUNTED by Elisabeth Naughton
An Eternal Guardians Novella

EYES ON YOU by Laura Kaye
A Blasphemy Novella

BLADE by Alexandra Ivy/Laura Wright
A Bayou Heat Novella

DRAGON BURN by Donna Grant
A Dark Kings Novella

TRIPPED OUT by Lorelei James
A Blacktop Cowboys® Novella

STUD FINDER by Lauren Blakely

MIDNIGHT UNLEASHED by Lara Adrian
A Midnight Breed Novella

HALLOW BE THE HAUNT by Heather Graham
A Krewe of Hunters Novella

DIRTY FILTHY FIX by Laurelin Paige
A Fixed Novella

THE BED MATE by Kendall Ryan
A Room Mate Novella

NIGHT GAMES by CD Reiss
A Games Novella

NO RESERVATIONS by Kristen Proby
A Fusion Novella

DAWN OF SURRENDER by Liliana Hart
A MacKenzie Family Novella

Discover 1001 Dark Nights Collection One

Go to www.1001DarkNights.com to subscribe.

FOREVER WICKED by Shayla Black
CRIMSON TWILIGHT by Heather Graham
CAPTURED IN SURRENDER by Liliana Hart
SILENT BITE: A SCANGUARDS WEDDING by Tina Folsom
DUNGEON GAMES by Lexi Blake
AZAGOTH by Larissa Ione
NEED YOU NOW by Lisa Renee Jones
SHOW ME, BABY by Cherise Sinclair
ROPED IN by Lorelei James
TEMPTED BY MIDNIGHT by Lara Adrian
THE FLAME by Christopher Rice
CARESS OF DARKNESS by Julie Kenner

Also from 1001 Dark Nights

TAME ME by J. Kenner

Discover 1001 Dark Nights Collection Two

Go to www.1001DarkNights.com to subscribe.

WICKED WOLF by Carrie Ann Ryan
WHEN IRISH EYES ARE HAUNTING by Heather Graham
EASY WITH YOU by Kristen Proby
MASTER OF FREEDOM by Cherise Sinclair
CARESS OF PLEASURE by Julie Kenner
ADORED by Lexi Blake
HADES by Larissa Ione
RAVAGED by Elisabeth Naughton
DREAM OF YOU by Jennifer L. Armentrout
STRIPPED DOWN by Lorelei James
RAGE/KILLIAN by Alexandra Ivy/Laura Wright
DRAGON KING by Donna Grant
PURE WICKED by Shayla Black
HARD AS STEEL by Laura Kaye
STROKE OF MIDNIGHT by Lara Adrian
ALL HALLOWS EVE by Heather Graham
KISS THE FLAME by Christopher Rice
DARING HER LOVE by Melissa Foster
TEASED by Rebecca Zanetti
THE PROMISE OF SURRENDER by Liliana Hart

Also from 1001 Dark Nights

THE SURRENDER GATE By Christopher Rice
SERVICING THE TARGET By Cherise Sinclair

Discover 1001 Dark Nights Collection Three

Go to www.1001DarkNights.com to subscribe.

HIDDEN INK by Carrie Ann Ryan
BLOOD ON THE BAYOU by Heather Graham
SEARCHING FOR MINE by Jennifer Probst
DANCE OF DESIRE by Christopher Rice
ROUGH RHYTHM by Tessa Bailey
DEVOTED by Lexi Blake
Z by Larissa Ione
FALLING UNDER YOU by Laurelin Paige
EASY FOR KEEPS by Kristen Proby
UNCHAINED by Elisabeth Naughton
HARD TO SERVE by Laura Kaye
DRAGON FEVER by Donna Grant
KAYDEN/SIMON by Alexandra Ivy/Laura Wright
STRUNG UP by Lorelei James
MIDNIGHT UNTAMED by Lara Adrian
TRICKED by Rebecca Zanetti
DIRTY WICKED by Shayla Black
THE ONLY ONE by Lauren Blakely
SWEET SURRENDER by Liliana Hart

About Heather Graham

New York Times and *USA Today* bestselling author, Heather Graham, majored in theater arts at the University of South Florida. After a stint of several years in dinner theater, back-up vocals, and bartending, she stayed home after the birth of her third child and began to write. Her first book was with Dell, and since then, she has written over two hundred novels and novellas including category, suspense, historical romance, vampire fiction, time travel, occult and Christmas family fare.

She is pleased to have been published in approximately twenty-five languages. She has written over 200 novels and has 60 million books in print. She has been honored with awards from booksellers and writers' organizations for excellence in her work, and she is also proud to be a recipient of the Silver Bullet from Thriller Writers and was also awarded the prestigious Thriller Master in 2016. She is also a recipient of the Lifetime Achievement Award from RWA. Heather has had books selected for the Doubleday Book Club and the Literary Guild, and has been quoted, interviewed, or featured in such publications as *The Nation, Redbook, Mystery Book Club, People* and *USA Today* and appeared on many newscasts including Today, Entertainment Tonight and local television.

Heather loves travel and anything that has to do with the water, and is a certified scuba diver. She also loves ballroom dancing. Each year she hosts the Vampire Ball and Dinner theater at the RT convention raising money for the Pediatric Aids Society and in 2006 she hosted the first Writers for New Orleans Workshop to benefit the stricken Gulf Region. She is also the founder of "The Slush Pile Players," presenting something that's "almost like entertainment" for various conferences and benefits. Married since high school graduation and the mother of five, her greatest love in life remains her family, but she also believes her career has been an incredible gift, and she is grateful every day to be doing something that she loves so very much for a living.

Discover More Heather Graham

Crimson Twilight: A Krewe of Hunters Novella

It's a happy time for Sloan Trent and Jane Everett. What could be happier than the event of their wedding? Their Krewe friends will all be there and the event will take place in a medieval castle transported brick by brick to the New England coast. Everyone is festive and thrilled... until the priest turns up dead just hours before the nuptials. Jane and Sloan must find the truth behind the man and the murder-- the secrets of the living and the dead--before they find themselves bound for eternity--not in wedded bliss but in the darkness of an historical wrong and their own brutal deaths.

* * * *

When Irish Eyes Are Haunting: A Krewe of Hunters Novella

Devin Lyle and Craig Rockwell are back, this time to a haunted castle in Ireland where a banshee may have gone wild—or maybe there's a much more rational explanation—one that involves a disgruntled heir, murder, and mayhem, all with that sexy light touch Heather Graham has turned into her trademark style.

* * * *

All Hallows Eve: A Krewe of Hunters Novella

Salem was a place near and dear to Jenny Duffy and Samuel Hall -- it was where they'd met on a strange and sinister case. They never dreamed that they'd be called back. That history could repeat itself in a most macabre and terrifying fashion. But, then again, it was Salem at Halloween. Seasoned Krewe members, they still find themselves facing the unspeakable horrors in a desperate race to save each other-and perhaps even their very souls.

* * * *

Blood on the Bayou: A Cafferty & Quinn Novella

It's winter and a chill has settled over the area near New Orleans, finding a stream of blood, a tourist follows it to a dead man, face down in the bayou.

The man has been done in by a vicious beating, so violent that his skull has been crushed in.

It's barely a day before a second victim is found... once again so badly thrashed that the water runs red. The city becomes riddled with fear.

An old family friend comes to Danni Cafferty, telling her that he's terrified, he's certain that he's received a message from the Blood Bayou killer--It's your turn to pay, blood on the bayou.

Cafferty and Quinn quickly become involved, and--as they all begin to realize that a gruesome local history is being repeated--they find themselves in a fight to save not just a friend, but, perhaps, their very own lives.

On behalf of 1001 Dark Nights,

Liz Berry and M.J. Rose would like to thank ~

Steve Berry
Doug Scofield
Kim Guidroz
Jillian Stein
InkSlinger PR
Dan Slater
Asha Hossain
Chris Graham
Fedora Chen
Kasi Alexander
Jessica Johns
Dylan Stockton
Richard Blake
BookTrib After Dark
and Simon Lipskar

50293768R00078

Made in the USA
Middletown, DE
28 October 2017